Tony,

Thank you for your p...

MW01168727

...In The Nick of Time

Everything is in God's Timing

by

LaSonya Jones-Lamine

authorHOUSE®

AuthorHouse™
1663 Liberty Drive, Suite 200
Bloomington, IN 47403
www.authorhouse.com
Phone: 1-800-839-8640

First published by AuthorHouse 6/19/2007

ISBN: 978-1-4259-9902-5 (sc)

Library of Congress Control Number: 2007903643

Printed in the United States of America
Bloomington, Indiana

This book is printed on acid-free paper.

57,924 words

Acknowledgments

I couldn't have written this novel without the help of my gracious God above who gave my mother, Dorothy, the writing talents so she could pass them on to me (thanks, Mom) my strong, loving husband Jeannet, who stands by me 100 percent in the goals I want to achieve: Thanks for being my true love, my first reader and my critic; and Anthony, my big brother, who shared his sword with me. The race is not to the swift, nor the battle to the strong, but to the one who endureth...right? Keep on trucking, big brother. Thanks to My sister Trina, who told me that if I can see it, I can do it; my poetically talented brother, Natambu, who has so many other talents it's unbelievable. It's your time to shine little brother. Believe that. And I give thanks last but not least to my daughter CheVaughn (Cookie) for being the designated babysitter while I breathed some air into this novel. I dedicate this book to you.

Introduction

I pray to the Lord, My soul to keep

With the purity of my attire and the sheer piece flowing flawlessly down my backside, I asked my God a question:

> **"Am I good enough to be received?"**
> ***And there was no answer.***

For most of my life, I have gone through series of events in which going through one door after another became a routine. On the other side of these doors that I am currently facing is something that will justify how well I did in my past. It will tell me how the rest of my life will turn out. Joy, happiness, and peace are all I have ever searched for. All I wanted in life was to be in a position where I didn't want to have to worry about a thing. Someone told me I could have that. *Dang!* I thought, *I could have that?*

> **"It sounds good, but what's the catch?" I said.**
> ***And there was no answer.***

My thoughts were in a serene, still, quiet, and tranquil place. I see footsteps through the sand, waves in clear blue water, and gold pavement below my feet. For my whole life, I have been going through dilemmas one after another, and now, I see peace.

> **"How can this be?" I said.**
> ***And there was no answer.***

Standing in front of a gorgeous, antiqued full-length vanity mirror, I took a long and hard glance at myself. In my reflection, I saw a strong and virtuous woman, yet I was in need of a perpetual circumstance in which I could be in harmony. For I know that I am a woman of faith, hope, power, and lots of courage. Let it be said and known that I still have yet another question remaining in my soul:

> **"When will you answer all my questions, Lord?"**
> ***And still…there was no answer.***

I took several deep breaths and released them harmoniously into the air. In a matter of moments I will be crossing over. And before I walk through those doors, there was something I was encouraged to understand through life's journey. It was for me to be prepared to give up all my old ways of living and renew my mind. Wait a minute! I have to give up everything? I don't know 'bout all this.

"What about my own personal dreams and goals?" I said.
And there was no answer.

I hunched my shoulders in faith that the answer would come sooner or later. And I was without a doubt in my mind that my journey has been fulfilled.

I stepped away from the beautiful full-bodied reflection of mine and froze. Wait! I need to take one last look at my self before I go. I looked back and thanked God that from this day forth, I had nothing else to worry about. All was said and done in the book of life.

Before walking toward the exit, I asked God another question:

"Nicole, what could you have done differently in your life?"
And I couldn't answer myself.

The knob on the door became my own personal symbol.
This doorknob represented the turning of a new beginning.
I reached my arm out nervously for the metal piece, clutching it tightly into the palm of my sweaty hands.
Nicole, the beautiful and quiet voice inside my head whispered, *I know you have had a rough life. I know all the things you tried to do; you thought you'd failed.*
My legs froze. I was receiving the answers in the nick of time because I was just about to walk out without a clue as to how to start my new journey. I knew I needed the answers first, so I opened my soul to listen.
I took the longest and deepest swallow I ever had and forced the air out of my nostrils. There was no way I was going to let my own impatience rush me into not hearing my answers. I stood behind the door, clutching the knob into my sweaty palms and waiting in silence.

"Once you walk through these doors, you'll realize that there is no turning back. Everything you needed already existed inside your heart. So walk through this door with your head up high and know that everything that has happened in your life was to make you stronger."

That voice is exactly what I needed to hear; now I'm confident.

As you continue this journey with me, picture each of these pages being a walk to your own door. Hold me in your spirit. Keep me close to the end. In the nick of time, it will all be revealed.

Take a walk through my life, and I will meet you at the last door. And we'll be able to open it together.

Chapter One

"I might look harmless."

My name is Nicole Salina Lewis, but my friends call me Nick—not ol' Saint Nick, not Nicky-Nick, but just Nick. Throughout my life, I have gone through a series of issues. Some of them may not be as bad as other people's are, but it was hard for me to cope because I didn't have anyone to turn to during my difficult moments. The worst part about being seventeen was that sometimes I had to use my body to get what I wanted. That was a bad choice for me. My body has always been used as a punching bag or a way to get what I want out of life more than anything. And I 'bout had enough of it. Now I want things to be different in my life. I don't want to end up dead like some of my friends or like the woman on the news who has been raped and beaten to death. I want strength.

My senior year in high school was the hardest. But in the end I was determined to get my life back on the right path sooner or later. I was not about to let these classes or any person stop me from reaching my goals.

I flunked two classes. I'm cool with that. There's always summer school. I won't be able to graduate with the rest of my classmates, but so what? As long as I can get my hands on a diploma, I can walk anywhere I want to after that. To hell with a stage.

My mother's name is Isis. It was her fault that I messed up in school in the first place. She is the type of person who is always right about everything, especially when she proposed that my life would end up in deep despair and maybe even suicide. She thought I was going to turn out to be a lesbian, take drugs, and flunk out of school. I wanted to prove her wrong. I had to. This was the only way I could get her to feel really stupid about the things she has been saying.

"I could care less if you lived or died." She would always say. She reminded me all the time about how much of a bastard child I was and how it was a mistake that I was born. Can you believe that? My own mother wished I was dead. This is why I called her by her real name, Isis (eye-sizz). I call her that because I feel that anyone who can birth a child and dog them doesn't deserve the honor of being called *Father* or *Mother*.

It all started when I had to serve time in the juvenile detention center. That is where I went after I had been released from jail. The way the system does things is a shame. They think that civilians should serve time a second time after they serve time the first time. That's like doing double for screwing up your own life in the first place. Oh how life sucks when we make the wrong decisions. And not only that, this juvenile record is stuck with me, like my big forehead, for the rest of my life.

I've been in juvenile detention centers several times, but this time was different. I had a fight with a girl named Cocoa whom everyone nicknamed Hoe-Hoe. She is the type that flirts and sleeps with each and every cute guy who enrolls in our school. Rumor had it that Cocoa wanted to see me about the newest guy, whose name was Alex. She said that if I didn't step back away from him, she was going to kick my ass. This is another case of another stupid chick trying to be barbaric and fight to get a man who doesn't want to be with her in the first place. And to top it all off, Alexander has a baby. I don't date anyone who's a *baby daddy* at this age. That's dangerous. However, I did promise I'd keep it a secret for him.

Oh yeah…back to the fight! I could have avoided the fight. I could've talked to a counselor and cleared this up. But no. I took all the steam my mother had been building up inside of me and released it on Cocoa's head.

Oh well. That's what she gets for messing with *Nicole Salina Lewis.*

I was in the gym, watching the men's basketball team practice when she approached me. I knew she was about to say something about the new guy in the school, but I saw a fight throbbing in her eyes. One thing led to another. She put her hands in my face. Before I knew it, I was being arrested for assault. They put Cocoa in an ambulance and me in a police car. It turned out that my quick-tempered self grabbed a baseball bat from the sports closet and beat her down with it. I can't remember any of that happening, but that's what my friend Jennifer told me. All I saw was black when she hit me. That's how I ended up in Juvenile. Even though I was happy to be released, going back home to this house of horror with Isis made me feel like crap.

I might look harmless. And some days, I may even be passive. But somewhere in life, everyone should grasp the old saying "Never judge a book by its cover." I don't dress like a hoochie mama, I don't need a crowd of loud-mouthed girls to hang with in order to justify myself, and I don't have all those colors in my hair like some punk rocker. I'm just an average, everyday teenager who wants to enjoy life and live it to the fullest.

"How did I become so sadistic?" I asked

Isis picked me up from the juvenile center. During the whole ride, she was silent. As we walked through the door, her frustration was released.

"Nicole Salina Lewis, I am so tired of you wasting my time," Isis said with a grudge as we entered the house. "It seems like the older you get, the more you seem like a waste of a life to me." She dropped her keys and purse onto the kitchen counter and began washing her hands.

I inhaled and then forcefully exhaled. I should have known this was coming

Chapter Two

"Going to jail was in good timing."

I've always hated explaining myself to my mother. She never wants to believe my side of the story. I thought of my mother as the strongest woman in the universe up until recently. There was a time when no one could tell me anything bad about her. I knew that my mother was my best friend. But now I feel differently. One thing I have grown to realize is that best friends don't put each other down for the lives they lead; they try to pull each other up and positively motivate and encourage each other. And for the last five years of my life, it's been hell trying to deal with my mother's negative ridicule.

"I didn't know that I was going to end up in juvenile again," I responded. "Cocoa started it and I finished it. It's not my fault she can't fight; she shouldn't have tried to fight me over a boy that's not hers in the first place."

I entered the house with my bags, took them up the stairs, and dropped them behind my bedroom door. I came back down the stairs and stood in the kitchen doorway where Isis was standing in the refrigerator.

"You know what Nicole? The day that you get a job and find your own place is the day that I will quit gambling," Isis said with simplicity. "Then you'd be outta my hair."

"You'd be outta mine too." I cold-heartedly mumbled under my breath.

"What in the hell did you just say?"

"Nothing," I sang. I forgot that Mom's ears were like satellites. "Is it okay if you take me to go and see about some jobs? I don't have any transportation."

"What's wrong with the bus?" Giving me a nondescript frown, she grabbed her car keys off the counter and dropped them into her purse as if I had plans to steal her old Honda Accord.

"I hate the bus. It's hard to go look for jobs on the bus," I told her as I grabbed an apple from the hanging fruit basket.

"Well that ain't my problem, Nicole. You just lazy, that's all. You sit around and wait for things to happen," She informed me while taking pots and pans out of the bottom cupboard and placing them on the stove.

I got good grades in school. I was always into school activities, such as band and the French club, and I did volunteer work for a nursing home at the beginning of the high school semester. It just makes me lose interest to know that I have to come home to this unconstructive criticism. Besides nagging me and getting drunk, my mother sits around waiting for her unemployment and welfare checks. Then she turns around and blames me for the reasons she has to accept them.

I took a big bite of my apple, taking my time to chew every morsel of this juicy red fruit. I am thinking about how strong and independent I am and how I can get my own money in my own way and not ask anybody for anything. Depending on how I feel at the time, I might turn a little trick here and there with the fellas just to make some quick money. Don't worry. I turn tricks like most women do. I find a man with some money, pretend I like him, give him a little of my time, watch him, seek, and destroy. Before I know it, I have new clothes and my hair, nails, and toes are done. And for those judgmental women who say that it's wrong…they probably don't have game anyway.

"You know you always been spoiled. You ain't gon' ever amount to nothing as far as I'm concerned," she said. She pulled a package of chicken from the refrigerator and pulled the plastic from it. "Didn't you just get through telling me that you were going to try to get yourself together?" she asked as she bent over to smell the packaged food.

I walked over and took a seat at the counter where she was preparing the food and bit into my juicy red apple again.

"Yes, I did tell you that, but like I said before, it was not my fault. She shouldn't have put her hands in my face."

"You act like you have no sense of control whatsoever, just like your daddy. You're stubborn, and don't want nobody to tell you nothing." she said. She took out a butcher knife from the drawer and began cutting the chicken breast into little pieces on the wooden cutting board. This was scary. For a moment, I thought she was going to throw it like a magician does to his blindfolded assistant. I thought it was my time to die.

"What are you so jumpy about?"

"I'm cool, I guess," I scoffed. My heart pounded, my eyebrows lifted, and the taste in my mouth had left the building.

I hated it when she spoke negatively about my father. I don't know my father that well. In fact, I don't even remember him. The only thing she tells me is that his first name is Gregory and his last name is Duncan and he lives far from here. The way she remembers him is that he never wanted to go anywhere or do anything when they were together, that he is nothing but trouble, and that he didn't want to be bothered with us anymore. Mom said that he left us when I was two and never looked back.

"Mama, I haven't lost my mind, I know where it's at."

"Well, since you know where it's at, shouldn't you find it and use it?" She asked as she put the cubed chicken into the already greased and heated skillet. If I could love Isis for one thing, it would be the way she cooked. She can throw down in the kitchen. On holidays, she cooks up a variety of foods and has all her fake friends over. She makes collard greens, macaroni and cheese, turkeys, potato salad, coleslaw, cornbread, candied yams, fried chicken, string beans, sweet potato pies, and peach cobbler. All her dishes are cooked and prepared from scratch. Why she never bothered to use her skills to cater or chef in some rich folk's kitchen is what I didn't understand.

"Uh-oh. here we go again." I mumbled. I rolled my eyes, bit my apple, threw the rest of it in the trash, and began walking out of the kitchen.

"See, that's what's wrong with you, Nicole. You run away every time somebody is trying to help you."

"I'm sorry if I don't see how putting someone down is helping me."

Before I could exit the aroma filled room the phone began ringing.

"Do you want me to get that for you, or should I ignore it?" I asked

"Just pick up the damn phone and stop trying to be a smart ass. You know you can't outsmart me."

"You don't have to get all cursy-cursy on me. I asked just in case you were hiding from bill collectors again."

As Isis rolled her eyes and smacked her teeth, I reached over to retrieve the ringing phone.

"Hello, who dis?"

"You have a collect call from the Jackson Correctional Facility. Will you accept the charges?" The faceless, squeaky-toned operator asked.

"It's Harold," I whispered disappointedly. Isis grabbed a towel from the dish rack, wiped her hands, and tossed the towel onto the counter top, from which it fell onto the floor.

"Give it to me," she demanded, trying to snatch the phone. I pulled back and threw up my index finger.

"Okay, okay," I said to Isis before turning my attention back to the faceless operator. "I would love to accept this call, but I don't like Harold. But I'm pretty sure that my mother will take it. She is the one who's going to let him run up her phone bill as usual. I am going to pass the phone to her, okay? Hold on, Ms. Operator."

As I was talking, Isis reached over my shoulder and snatched the phone from my hands. I let out an enormous laugh.

"Nicole, you just won't quit, will you? Why don't you go and clean your room until our chicken fajitas are done, will you?"

"I think that I'll go and draw a picture of Harold and throw darts at it instead. How does that sound?" I flashed her a fake smile and walked out of the kitchen door, making sure I was close enough to hear their conversation.

"Hello. Hey baby, what's going on? Well, how much do you need?Oh yeah, I can do that for you; that's not a problem. Okay. Love you too, baby. See you soon. 'Bye.

When her conversation with the Harold ended, she slammed the phone onto the hook. "He is always asking for stuff."

Harold is the boyfriend. He is serving time for armed robbery and assault. He was trying to rob a liquor store with a stolen weapon, but the police caught him. He also has this habit of borrowing money from a loan shark named Jet-Money and not paying it back on time. Robbing a liquor store, getting caught, and winding up in jail caused his payments to be late. So not only is he serving time for robbery, but he also became target practice for Jet-Money and his boys when he is released, because he still doesn't have the money he owes. How stupid is this criminal?

After dinner, I was dying to hear what people were saying about the fight I had with Cocoa in school. I had to know if I was the talk of the week. Hell, I put a girl in an ambulance for Christ's sake, and the whole school saw it.

I jumped in the shower, put on my flannel pajamas, grabbed my pedicure case, and sat down on my bed. I picked up the phone and called my girl, Jennifer, up. Jennifer used to stay across the street from me. Her mother, Ms. Taylor, has a lot of schoolbook knowledge as well as biblical knowledge. Since her mom graduated, landed a good job at Chrysler, and moved into a better neighborhood, we hadn't been talking as much as we used to. But lucky for me, we still attend the same school. Their house was always a place to go when Isis and I had our disputes. Jennifer's mother finished college, got her degree, landed a good job, packed up, and moved to Bloomfield Hills. There are some of the nicest, biggest, and most expensive houses in Bloomfield Hills. Ever since she left me two years ago, it's been pretty rough around here for me. We still go to the same school, but I hardly ever get a chance to talk to her like we used to talk.

I remember when she held bake sales at her church. She did this in order to support herself and pay tuition. I was never into going to the church services, but I would come just to get my share of the sweets.

I picked up the phone in my room and dialed her number.

"Hello," she answered.

"What up Jen, what you been up to?" I asked.

"Nothin'. Just trying to help my mother with the laundry. I was thinking about you earlier and I started to call you," she explained

"Girl, we usually do that to each other, don't we?"

"Do what?"

"Think of each other at the same time," I answered

"Oh yeah, I know. Now that could be a sign."

"What kind of sign is that?" I asked. "We're just two people thinking of something at the same time. We hardly talked in school, and ever since you moved across the country, it's been even harder to talk to you."

"Yeah, yeah. True dat, true dat," She said, sounding like she was really meditating on that. "But I didn't move across country, though. Besides, it's only a twenty minute drive from you."

"Yeah, but tell me how long of a walk is it? You know I don't have a car."

We both snickered.

"So, tell me what's been going on since I've been gone." I said.

She took a deep breath. "Well, remember the guy that used to come by and cut my brother's hair all the time?"

I nodded my head and then answered. "Uh-huh, Clarence. What about him?"

"Girl, he got killed."

"Ren died?" I shouted. I slammed the fingernail file down on my vanity so hard that my nail polish tray bounced and rolled onto the floor. I didn't care to pick it up. Clarence was my sweetheart. We used to have our little bump and grind sessions back in the day. We occasionally messed around on the down low from time to time. Of course, Jennifer never knew about us.

"Did you just say Ren got killed?" I asked, holding my chest with my hand.

"Yep, Clarence died last Tuesday. He got shot at the movie theater. He had two bullets in his chest."

"Oh my God. Why didn't you tell me?"

"I am telling you now that he is dead!"

"I mean why didn't you tell me right after you found out?" I tried not to let her hear the tears in my voice over the phone. But it was too late. My voice was already wiggling with sadness.

"That's because I have been trying to contact you since it happened," she said, sounding investigative. "And exactly where have you been? I have been trying to call you, and not even your mother would answer the phone. You should think about getting a cell phone."

Did Jennifer know that I had been put in jail for that fight? Did she know that Clarence got me pregnant when I was fifteen years old? Did she know about the abortion? I didn't think that it was a good idea to tell her that I had been messing around with him, but that didn't keep me from seeing him. I would rather not sneak around and do it, but I knew that Jennifer would not have approved of it. Therefore, Clarence and I kept it a secret.

"He was cool. Hate to see a good man go down," I said, wiping the tears from my eyes and brushing them onto the pants of my flannel pajamas.

"Oh yeah, I know," she remarked.

Silence grew between us. Her breaths became heavier and faster. The ticking clock in the background became louder. Finally, her voice mellowed through the phone's earpiece.

"When are you coming back to school?"

"I'm not sure. I have to call the office and find out. Plus, I haven't been feeling good lately."

"What do you think it's from?" she asked

"Just menstruating and stuff. Got headaches and everything," I said in a sickly tone.

"Oh." Jennifer said "Well I hope you feel better soon."

"Thanks."

"Well anyway, I better get off this phone so I can catch up on my chores," she said in a serious tone. "Can I call you back later after I am done."

"Oh yeah. Tell Ms. Taylor I said hello, too."

"I'll tell her."

"Okay, Jenny," I said with a stretch and yawn, "we will talk more later."

"Oh yeah," she said. "Most definitely."

Then we hung up without a word as to what people were saying about the fight I had been in.

Damn. My first real boyfriend—shot and killed.

Wait a minute. Clarence and I were supposed to go to that movie together. I could have been with him when it happened. So going to jail might have actually been a good thing. I was put in jail in the nick of time. I could have been dead along with him.

Chapter Three

"Never leave home without it."

"Nicole, Get your lazy behind outta bed and come down here. You got company," my mother yelled as she stood at the bottom of the stairs, banging on the banister. "And don't have 'em waiting too long, either."

When I was growing up, banging on the rail and shouting piercingly was how she would wake me up for school. I hated it then, and I hate it even worse today.

"Who is it?" I loudly asked.

"You need to bring your lazy ass down here and see for yourself," she snapped.

I had to stop, inhale, and exhale for a moment. I wanted to say something sarcastic, but I knew that if I did, it would have sent her up the stairs and into my room, bringing drastic measures. So I held my peace.

"Well, could you please tell them that I'll be down in a minute?" I politely asked. But I received no reply from her. It makes me wonder if she will ever get up on the right side of bed. And if she does get up happy, I want to know what it was that made her that way so I can invest in it.

Rising from my bed and making my way to the vanity mirror, I brushed my curly, shoulder-length hair and tied it into a scrunchie. The aroma of a man's cologne lurked through the living room and up the stairs, making its way through the cracks in my bedroom door. I can smell a man's cologne in the air from miles away.

Sniff sniff. That smells like my boyfriend Mike downstairs waiting for me.

As I scurried around the room looking for something more satisfying to wear, my pinky toe hit the corner of my bed slats, splitting my skin open like a peach.

"Ow! Shit!"

After taking several breaths to release the pain, I stuck my head around my bedroom door and hollered. "Mike, baby, I'll be down in a few minutes." I heard noises, but I didn't get a response.

While cautiously sliding my sore feet into a gauze and placing my short thick legs into favorite denims, I put on my favorite pocketed hooded sweatshirt. I thought about how much of a pain in the neck my "Cash-Money" Mike could be. But what else could I expect from a twenty-five year old who saw his parents executed in their own home?

Mike's parents owed Jet-Money some money. He told me that when he was seven years old, he was in the back room playing video games and heard gunshots coming from the front room. He grabbed the cordless phone, hid in the closet, and called 911. When the police arrived thirty minutes later, Mike went into the front room to open the door and found his mother and father's wounded bodies in the middle of the livingroom floor. He told me that he has flashbacks of his mother's bloody head and the bone of his father's leg from time to time. Mike was placed under the care of his grandmother, who is now deceased. Grandma Pearl died when he was thirteen years old, which led Mike to live in the streets.

After he shared that information with me, I realized something: He needed someone to show him love even when he refused to accept it.

After getting dressed, I stepped out of my bedroom door and walked gracefully down the staircase and into the living room where he stood. *I'm glad he's here,* I thought, *'cause Mike sells drugs. He could help me through the midst of my financial difficulties.*

"Hey handsome," I whispered, blowing an imaginary kiss in the air. I wrapped my arms around his neck, kissing the side of his lips. He was looking good, too. He had on a New York Knicks jersey with a matching hat, his two-tone brushed jeans, and some white kicks. His gold chain, which said "Mike" in diamonds, hung on his chest, and along with the gold watch and diamond earring, it made him look even more delicious.

"Where in the hell have you been?" He forcefully whispered. His face was hardened and his eyes were bloodshot. "I told you once before about disappearing on me like this, Nikki."

"Why you got to call me Nikki? You know I hate that name," I whined with a frown on my face, lightly pushing him away. "And I was busy doing my own thang. I thought that you'd be happy to see me."

"Fuck that. You still haven't answered my question." His hands were giving me the gangsta-style theatrical attention I despised. He grabbed my arm so tightly that my blood stopped its circulation and my hand became limp and numb. "I asked you where you been all this time?"

"Boy, whatever," I said, releasing my arm from his clutch. I folded my arms and took a step back. He took a step toward me and grabbed me by my neck.

"Uh-uh. See, you got me confused with somebody else. Don't "whatever" me. You think this is a game, don't you?" while grabbing my neck, he pressed his trigger finger into the middle of my forehead, like a gun. "I asked you where the hell you been, and I want an answer."

I turned my head to see if Isis's timing would allow her to walk up the stairs and witness this awful act of his. At least this would have given me the chance to release myself from his demonic clutch.

"C'mon Mike. Let me go."

"Oh, now you know my name. For a second there I thought you forgot who I was," he said as he pushed my head away with his fingers and released my neck.

"No, I didn't," I said to him, trying to gain my composure. "And why are you acting this way? Coming over here and acting like you my daddy," I said to him as I tried to straighten my clothes. This punk had a tight grip on me, and his demonic look was scary. I should have grabbed the naked statue that Isis had on the coffee table and hit him over the head with it. But I remembered that I needed money.

"I'm trying to get my money right, and you up in some other nigga's face. I got goals to achieve, and you playing hide-and-go-seek."

I stepped forward and grabbed his hands. "Baby? Baby? Come on, now. I know you didn't come over here just to argue; you know you my man. So what you need me to do?" I said, kissing him on the chest just to calm him down.

"You need to recognize who you messing with," He said just before Isis barged up from the basement door.

Isis missed it. She never gets to see the bad side of Mike. She believes that anything Mike says is legit. She thinks that he is an immaculate man who knows how to handle his business. I must admit, Mike does handle his business, but I don't think she really knows what kind of business Mike is really into. And even though Mike has a lot of schoolboy sense, he refuses to go to school. He prefers to make his money now rather than getting an honest job. He says his personality changes too much to work a nine to five job.

"So what kind of plans you two lovebirds got going on?" she interrupted, dropping a basket full of clothes on the living room floor and plopping onto the plastic covered couch.

"Ms. Lewis, Nicole and I are going out to breakfast. Would you like to go with us?" he said, sounding courteous. I knew he was going to change into his other personality. I just knew it.

"That is so sweet of you, but I will have to pass. You see, my house looks a mess. Nicole was supposed to do this this morning, but if you take her with you, that would be better for me. As a matter of fact, why don't you let her move in with you. She don't do much around here anyway but eat, sleep, and shit."

I gave her a cold stare, but I kept quiet. I wanted to see how far she was going to go this time.

Mike's pager vibrated on his cell phone. He unhooked it from his belt, scanned it to see the number, and snapped it back on his belt.

"Well, I wish she could. You know she would be in good hands, don't you?" He asked. He glanced at me with a sneaky smirk on his face.

"Humph," I scoffed. I wonder if she would continue to push me off on him if she only knew of Mike's other side. It might be better if I ran off with him. I could put up with his stuff better than I could hers. Then again, I might be putting myself in more danger.

Mike's pager vibrated on his cell for the second time.

Isis started to say something about the pager, but I cut her off.

"I'm just trying to get my grub on, so can we go? Please?" I looked at him and smiled.

He turned to my mother and said, "Oh, sure thing sweetheart. If you will excuse us, Ms. Lewis?" He grabbed my hand and led me toward the door. Thank God I left my slip on shoes close to the door. The way he pulled me, he must not have noticed that my feet were naked. I hopped into my pink slip-on K-Swiss gym shoes so fast that it caused me to stumble. I'm surprised I had time to snatch my house keys off of the hook at the same time I put my shoes on.

"So I guess I'll have to leave the light on for you, huh Nicole?" Isis asked, giving me a wink of the eye like a sailor on a voyage.

Mike grabbed the doorknob. "Yeah, why don't you do that for her. Thanks, Ms. Lewis." he said hurriedly, closing the door behind us.

We jumped into his black Escalade and drove downtown to our favorite restaurant. We usually eat at Gina's Steak and Waffles when we are celebrating—especially when Mike has come up with a plan that will bring him into lump sums of money.

When we got to our table, I ordered my usual: a sausage, egg, and cheese omelet with an orange juice. He ordered a steak, pancakes, hash browns, and eggs with an orange juice. He finished his breakfast before I could taste and chew my first bite.

After he took his last bite, he threw his fork down, took a swig of his juice, looked around the room, and forcefully asked, "So, peep dis, Nick. I need you to make a delivery for me. You think you can handle that?"

I looked up from my plate and dropped my fork into it. I've never had to go with him to do a delivery before. To me, those are dangerous. I thrive on excitement, and he knew it. But going inside of some crack house where they manufacture the product was the last thing I would do to get some money.

"What kind of delivery? And when?" I asked, pretending that I had no idea what he was talking about.

"I have something I need for you to drop off. When he gives you what you should have, you take what he gives you. Then you bounce up outta there. Easiest money you will ever make. Don't waste your time bumpin' yo' gums. All that small talk ain't even necessary."

"How much money are we talking about?"

"For you?"

"Yeah, for me"

"I don't know. How much you need?"

"How much you willing to give?"

"$300."

I sat back in my chair and dropped my head back against the booth's chair. "Mike, you know $300 is not enough for a job like that. And plus, I don't feel good about this. I never did one of these before, but I hear the horror stories about going into these houses all the time," I said to him. "And in the meantime, where are you going be at?"

"I will be close by with my heat, baby. You know I won't let anything happen to you. You believe me, don't you?"

"Yeah, I believe you." I leaned forward, taking another swig of my orange juice. "So when do you need this done?"

Now I'm in shame. How did that question come out of my mouth?

"Like, in the next twenty minutes," he answered. "The dude who kept blowin' up my pager at ' your moms crib was the one who needs it."

Mike didn't waste time. I wasn't expecting to do it this early. I wished he would at least wait until the sun fully came out and shined on a corner of the earth first.

"Okay…I'll do it," I said. I needed money. And if this was what I had to do, then so be it.

Mike paused for a moment. He looked up over my plate and into the vicinity of my breast. He gave me an awkward look, as if I had a big piece of parsley leaf hanging from my nose.

"What's wrong with you?" I asked

"Where in the hell is your bra?" he asked, keeping his eyes on my braless breasts. "Did you know that everybody can see your nipples poking through your shirt?

I chuckled "You know what? Everything happened so fast, I didn't have time to put one on," I said to him.

"You got on panties?" He frowned. He scooted his chair back and looked under the table.

"No," I answered, drawing an imaginary circle on the tablecloth with my fingers. "As a matter of fact, I don't. Why you ask? You want to see it?"

"Ugh, you nasty!" He grabbed a used napkin and threw it across the table. It hit my chin and landed on my plate.

We both laughed it off. Even though he had put his hand around my neck earlier and had embarrassed me in front of the other people in the restaurant, it was good to see him laughing again.

***"I want to give my support, but am I giving the right kind?" I said.
And I waited patiently for the answer***

Chapter Four

"You will not be handed over to those you fear."
Jeremiah 39:17

The ride to the drop house was quick. Mike hardly spoke a word to me after we left the restaurant.

"Aight Nick, you know what to do, baby. Go and handle yourself like a real woman." Mike put the truck in park, reached underneath the back of my seat, and pulled out a small duffel bag.

"I got this," I said, reassuring him. I opened the door and walked up the walkway nervously, like an old woman with hip problems.

A man—A big man who weighed almost a ton, opened the door for me as if I was a VIP. He was the ugliest man I had ever seen. His arms hung hugely at his sides like an ape's, and his face looked like someone had let the cats use it for a scratching post. His eyes were cocked, his shoes were torn and his body odor reeked of rotten potatoes.

Entering through the front door, three men sat haughtily in the front room with holsters hanging on their sides. The table they sat at was full of cash and crack that was wrapped in plastic packaging. Over to my left was a woman who was dressed in an elegant evening gown. Her hair, nails, and make up were coordinated with her ensemble. She was as pretty as Tyra Banks without the innocent look. I have known women who possessed that type of appearance. She was the type that would get your arm blown off if you got in the way of her man or her money. She had the kind of look that showed she didn't care about friendships or family, but just money.

The large bouncer took me toward the back of the house. Women were prepping the drugs in one room, and men were torturing a man by the neck in another room. This house was bigger than it looked from the outside, and this was more than I had expected a drop house to be.

"You got what I need?" a thunderous voice asked. The roar in his tone snapped me back into reality rather quickly. The fat bouncer snatched the bag from my hands and threw it on the table in front of "Mr. Big." I stood in the same position, watching in fear as he searched the bag. First, he unzipped it and paused. Then he flipped through what was in the bag and looked up at me. Mr. Big laughed wickedly before pulling a .22-caliber pistol from his desk and placing it on the desktop. He then pulled out a wad of money. He counted it, separated it, tucked the extra money back into his drawer, and closed the drawer shut. He reached over to zip the bag and dropped it onto the floor next to his chair.

"You tight, boss?" the fat bouncer asked.

"It's all there," Mr. Big said to the oversized bouncer. Before giving him the money, he stared my body up and down and then gave me a left-eyed wink. The bouncer took the money and tossed it in my direction. It hit the floor with a thud.

"Well aren't you going to pick it up?" The bouncer asked

Without saying a word, I bent over to pick up cash and the bouncer's laid his hand upon my butt, and began moving it in a soft circular motion.

"Hey! what the hell are you doing?" I asked

"Yeah, I did it, and what are you going to do about it?"

I was too scared. I gave him a dirty look, grabbed the money, and headed out of the room.

Three gunshots came from another room. Mr. Big jumped out of his chair. He grabbed his Glock from the desk, then gave me the "Our-work-is-done-here-now-get-lost" look. I tucked the money in my front pocket and headed back toward the front door.

At the front door was a man who was shooting at the men with the holsters. He forced the door open and pushed himself in. I turned around and ran into the opposite direction. He begin shooting at me.

Anxiously looking for another portal to run through, I thought my life was over. With the bullets coming from so many directions, the only thing I could do was duck and dodge. In the meantime, I kept my mind in prayer.

"Lord, I didn't know what I was walking into. Could you please lead me out of this alive?"
This time, the answer was quick.

I was desperate. I was trying to get out the same way I had come in, but it didn't work. I turned around and began running towards the other rooms.

I found a half opened window from one of the bedroom's, and dove through it. I heard the bullets whizzing past my ears. And in spite of the bullets and chairs that flew past my ears, nothing touched me. I took a breath. Overjoyed to see Mike's truck parked along the curbside.

"Mike pull off, now!" I shouted, jumping into the truck and slamming the door. Mike snapped the truck into drive and pulled off.

"Did you get the money is all I want to know."

"Here, take it!" I reached into my sweatshirt pocket and pulled out the wad of money.

"Don't pull it out now, are you crazy?" he pushed my hand and the money back into my sweatshirt pocket. "You don't pass me no money until we clear from the area. Is that understood?"

"Mike don't ask me to do this again. It's too much for me."

"What are you talking about? I know you're not scared of a few bullets?"

"Bullets kill, Mike. I could've gotten killed in there." I yelled nervously.

After he finished laughing hysterically, all he could say was "But you didn't."

"This shit isn't funny, dog. For all you know, I could have had a bullet in me right now." I said to him

"Why you think I sent you to do it for me? I can't take any more of that either. That's why I need you to get it for me from now on," he said. He grabbed my chin and flashed me the dirtiest grin.

"So you know what goes on in there the majority of the time and you insist I go in for you?" I asked, desperately awaiting his answer. But he didn't reply.

"Stop trippin'. I knew you was gon' be aight. It don't pop off like that all the time. Only when somebody is trying to get over on somebody else," He said to me as if it was no big deal. It seemed like Mike didn't care about anyone's life but his own. This was really not worth $300.

Mike pulled his Escalade into a vacant parking lot and put it into park.

"Aight, look. You gotta trust me. You just so happened to walk in there at the wrong time, but you didn't get hurt. I hope that it doesn't mean you can't do it for me from now on. I'll give you five hundred dollars every time you go in instead of the usual three." He leaned toward me and stared at the side of my face. My eyes were focused on the unmoving windshield wipers that lay across his windshield. I did not want to look into his demonic eyes.

"But Mike—"

"But what?" he interrupted. He reached down into the ashtray and pulled out a blunt. He lit it, took a puff and held it in his breath as he spoke. "Now, If you gon' be my woman, you need to look out for me and do this, aight? Nah, that's it. No more discussion about it," he said dominantly. "If you are going be my woman Nick, this is what comes with it. You either roll with it or you don't."

I didn't want to do this, but I didn't want him to think I wasn't fit to be his woman.

He blew the smoke out my direction. "So what day do you plan to reach into your pocket and pull out my money?" Mike asked just before his left temple was introduced by a 12 gauge shotgun.

"Even if you tried to move, I got a partner over there that'll blow your woman's head across that dashboard," the gun holder said.

"Aight, man, aight, be cool. Just let her go. I'm not—"

"Shut the hell up! Ain't nobody ask you anything," The gun holder said, poking the gun into his head. Mike's head shook with every syllable the gunman expressed. "You know what I'm here for, Mike. Don't you owe Jet-Money something?"

"I got it dawg. Straight up. It's in the trunk." Mike said.

The gunman allowed Mike to hit the trunk button. A second gunman went to the trunk, opened it, and pulled out suitcases. A third gunman opened my door and snatched me out. I jumped out the car wondering just how much Mike had borrowed from Jet-Money and hoping it was all there so we could all go home alive. Everyone knows not to mess with Jet-Money and his money. The only thing I could think of at a time like this was my mother, believe it or not.

"Why don't you just come with me?" My gunman demanded. He dragged me by the hair away from Mike's truck and tossed me to the ground. My face fell into the pebbly pavement and I bumped my forehead against a sharp rock.

"Ouch!" I shouted. Now my forehead was throbbing. Before I knew it, there was blood trickling off of my forehead and snow skiing it's way down my nose.

I couldn't see what was going on with Mike because my back was turned. The dust and blood that were layered on my face distracted my vision. And plus, I dared not to move. I could feel the nose of the gun pointing into the back of my head.

"Please don't hurt me," I quietly cried as I cupped my hands behind my head.

"Just shut up and don't move!" The gunman said, forcing his words out, and pushing the gun harder into my head. "This ain't got nothing to do with you unless you want it to."

There were three gunshots I heard from behind. I screamed. I closed my eyes, buried my face inside the broken rocky pavement, and waited for my turn to come.

"Let's be out!" a grungy voice shouted.

"Stay on the ground pretty lady, and don't you move or you dead too," he commanded. I listened.

I lay face down on the ground until I heard the sounds of their vehicles fade away.

I looked back before jumping to my feet. I ran toward the truck. "Mike! Oh my God, what happened?"

The closer I got to the truck, the more I saw Mike gasping for air. He was completely covered in blood.

"Oh my God!" I shouted. "Could somebody please help me!?"

I held his hand. That was the only part of him that wasn't bloody. "Come on, Mike, you're going to make it! Dammit! Could somebody fucking help me here!?" I hollered from the top of my lungs, but no one responded.

Mike tried to speak, but his words made no sense. It was too late. He took his last breath before my very eyes, and his hand fell limply into mine.

I fell to my knees and cried. I knew that if I stuck around, the police would wonder why I had a stack of cash in my pocket. Then I would look guilty. They also left a gun in the passenger seat. It was a .357 magnum. Though the thought of me leaving Mike lying there made me feel even more horrible, I walked off, leaving his body soaking in his own blood.

Finally, after an hour of the scariest and most dreadful walking I had ever done, I came to my street. I noticed Isis's car wasn't in the driveway. Thank God!

"Isis! Are you in here?" I yelled, making sure neither she nor anyone else was in there before making my way into the house. Without hesitation, I made sure all the doors and windows were tightly secured, and I set the alarm. I went into the bedroom, took out the money from Mike's drop, then placed it on the bed.

I think it would be a good idea to put all this money under this mattress. I don't think it's a good idea to walk around here with all this on me, I thought. *Just keep some in your pocket just in case, but count it first.*

$10,000 in cash. Damn! Is this a fucking joke or what?

Separating $500 to the side and tucking the rest in my mattress set, I became nervous. While glancing at my shaking palms, I wondered just how much trouble I could get into if I was to get caught. Especially after touching Mike. I knew that there had to be some of his blood on me, or at least some fingerprints in the car. So now my best bet was to take a shower, get rid of these clothes, and clean the wound on my head.

I stopped to take a look in the mirror. Since Mike had come into this house, I'd brutally scarred my baby toe, nearly peeling the skin from it, my forehead had dried up blood on it that I thanked God no one was able to see, and my booty had been smacked by a greasy total stranger. What a day.

I put my clothes into a garbage bag and placed it deep inside the dumpster in the backyard. After my shower, I put on my low-riding denim blue jeans and a red t-shirt with the glittery words "Shorty" on it and lay across my bed. I was scared. I looked out my bedroom window several times in fear of the police walking up to my front porch to handcuff me and take me to prison.

The ringing of the phone scared me shitless. It frightened me so badly that I let out the biggest gas bubble my stomach could have held. And boy was it explosive.

I plopped down in the vanity mirror seat. "I hope this isn't the police. What if someone saw me walking away from Mike's murder and told the police?" I took a deep breath and looked at the caller ID. Jennifer Taylor's name flashed on the screen. Hesitating whether I should answer it, I took a deep breath and picked up the phone.

"Hello,"

"Nick, where have you been? I been trying to call you for over an hour now. You need to get you a cell phone or something, 'cause I have been trying to get in contact with you and you don't never be around. Did you know you were the hardest person to get ahold of?" she asked.

I was silent. I swear Jennifer acts just like a mother. At least we knew that her kids were going to be in check all the time. Poor things. "What is it Jenny? I'm kind of busy."

"Not too busy for this," she said. "Turn on channel eight news; it's yo' boy Mike."

I gasped and did a flying leap across my bed for the remote, which was lying on the nightstand. I pressed the power button to turn it on.

"They found Mike's body."

"Um Jenny?"

"Yeah?"

"Let me call you back," I hung the phone up.

The news reporters didn't mention anything about me. In fact, out of all the people who had interviews, no one said they saw another person with him. No one heard gunshots or knew anything. The persons who found Mike's body were two thirteen-year-old boys who were skipping school. The police had no leads, fingerprints, or clues left to prove who did it. I grabbed the remote and turned the television off and lay on my bed in silence.

I shed many tears. I shed some tears of fear because I could have died.

I shed some tears of loneliness because Mike will no longer be by my side.

I shed some tears of sadness because now he's long gone.

I shed some tears of anxiety because I might have been in the wrong.

Some tears were shed out of joy because I made it through.

I shed some of the tears out of hopelessness because there was nothing that I could do.

I can say this: When I got done crying all those tears, I was thinking about the 9,500 dollars' worth of tears that were going to be shed from my mattress set. And it's all mine. I wanted to get the money out and play with it again, but it would be just my luck that Isis or the police would pop in and catch me fondling it.

I stayed in my room for the rest of the day. I lay down on the bed until my eyes became heavy, and then I drifted to sleep.

Chapter Five

"The nuisance of a vicious cycle."

At the same time the sun was settling into the earth's atmosphere, one of Isis's creations in the air awakened me. The air was breezy, yet warm. I stepped out of bed, stretching my legs and fixing the blanket on my queen sized comfort zone. I looked up at the clock and noticed that I had been asleep for the largest part of the evening. Was it six o'clock in the evening already?

After modeling in the mirror and giving myself a double check in regard to my attire, the aroma of green peppers and onions led my nose down to the kitchen and into the pot.

"Yup yup uh. Wuh wuh uh. Yup to the yup and uh to the uh. Chill-ay everybody Say chill-ay."

After dancing my way to the cupboard for the biggest bowl I could find and to the silverware drawer for the biggest spoon there was, I helped myself to the delicious mixture of chili and the crackers from the countertop.

"Nicole, what happened to Mike?" Isis's voice blurted from the other side of the kitchen wall.

"I don't know. What did you hear?" I asked in return with the thought of that monster nightmare being a dream. I was almost sure that that scene didn't exist until she said his name. After that, my mood for this homemade chili went straight to hell.

"Well I heard on the news that he got shot."

"Yeah, um, that's what I heard too."

Please Isis, don't come into the kitchen. The word "guilt" is written all over my face and you don't need to see it.

"Where were you when this happened?" she asked from afar.

"Um, I was here." I said

I heard the plastic from the couch covers move, so I knew she was on her way into the kitchen. My first thought was to wipe the words "I know what happened to Mike." off of my forehead.

After a couple of heavy footsteps, she stumbled into the room. She was drunk.

"You been locked up in that room all this time, huh?"

"Yup." I answered into the bowl of chili while trying to keep my eyes from meeting with hers.

"How come you lockin' yourself up like somebody is after you? I came in and the alarm was on and all the windows were locked up. Are you in some kind of trouble again? And what the hell is that big Band-Aid doing on your forehead? I told you, if you get into any more trouble, I am going to m—"

"No, I'm not in no kind of trouble," I said while stacking up a pile of meat on my spoon and lifting it into my mouth. It was very hard to swallow with the huge lump that was already stuck in my throat. "And this scratch on my forehead is just an acne bump. It's nothing."

"You know what? I don't care if someone knocked you in your head or your head exploded. Mike is dead and I didn't know if you were kidnapped or dead too," she said.

"Why would you think I was kidnapped? Didn't you say that you came home and the alarm was on? I think you knew I was upstairs." I said while taking another tablespoon of chili.

"You are always pulling tricks like this, Nicole. You go away and don't come back for days. Sometimes I just wish you would just get your stuff and move the hell outta here. You' re driving me crazy."

What a shame. My mother was always getting drunk and finding something to argue about. She has a history of doing this to me. I was usually the one to get choked when we went through this. But staying around long enough for her to go through the same vicious cycle again is becoming a nuisance. I hope she doesn't push that button today. Hell, I just lost Mike, and I could've died. I don't think her putting her hands on me would be a good idea right now.

"Mike dropped me off from down the street, and I walked the rest of the way. That's the last time I saw Mike," I explained.

"You were the last person with Mike. They're probably trying to look for you now. I tell you Nicole, this makes no sense how I raised one child, gave her everything, and she still winds up making the most craziest decisions." She stood there shaking her head before screaming at the top of her lungs. "Why is Mike dead?!"

"Momma, I don't know what happened to him, okay? And why are you so worried about him anyways, what's he ever done for you?"

"Well, for one thing, he's my dealer. I didn't have money one day he sold me a quarter. That's when him and I became sexually involved. And yes, I think it's about time you knew that."

Sexually involved? Sexually involved? Did she just say sexually involved?

I dropped the spoon into my bowl and pushed it in the center of the table. "So now I'm collateral? Is that why you kept pushing him onto me? How long were you planning on letting this go on? Until Harold gets out of jail?"

She moved closer to me and grabbed my collar. Putting her fingers in my face, she said, "Did I just hear you call me stupid?"

"No I did not. You're drunk. Can't we talk about this when you're sober," I told her, waving her hand out of my face.

"This is my house. When was the last time you helped me pay a bill? I had to get my money from somewhere."

"Whether I pay bills or not, I think I have a right to know how you're using me for collateral," I declared.

Before I could get the words out, she had her arm cocked back into position. Her arm came down, giving me her famous right hook into my jaw. I hit the floor with a thud, thrashing the back of my head on the cabinet on the way down. When the ringing in my ear stopped after the impact, I stood on my feet. I couldn't believe this; Isis was the one in the wrong and I was the one who got knocked onto the kitchen floor.

"What the hell did you do that for?" I said, screaming from the top of my lungs and still holding my jaw.

She pointed her finger at my nose. "Nicole, You are always into some mess. What if somebody comes looking for you and comes after me, too? Then what?"

I no longer cared about her, Harold, or Mike's dirty ass. My only thought was, *What would she do if I hauled off, cocked my arm back and gave her a hook into her jaw? The police would be here, hooking me up to those metal rings, and placing me under arrest again. If I'm lucky, they just might search my room and find all the money I got, and somehow connect it to Mike's murder.* So, to avoid all the drama and the to-be-continued episodes, I went with the most mature thing.

"You know what? I'm outta here," I said, heading toward the steps. Isis ran behind me and shoved me. I fell and bumped my chin on the stair railing.

"They should've taken your life instead of his."

"I don't have to stay here and take this," I said, struggling to get my painful body off the floor and up the stairs.

"That's all you ever do is take stuff anyway, you little tramp!"

While I packed my clothes into my duffle bag, she talked and murmured to herself from the floor beneath me. After packing four changes of clothes, house keys, my wallet, and the picture of my father my duffle bag, I stormed down the steps and out of the front door and walked until I reached the end of the block. That was when I stopped to check my pockets, realizing they were 9,500 dollars short.

Dammit! I forgot about my money in the mattress. I'm sure it'll be safe there. I will wait until all of this blows over. Then she will let me move back in. I thought to myself.

While I was circling around the block, Jennifer popped into my mind. I stopped by the pay phone and dialed Jenny's phone number, hoping she was still home.

"Hello," Jenny said.

"Jenny…boy am I glad you're still at the house."

"Yeah, I'm still here. I was starting to worry about you since you hung up on me earlier."

"I know Jenny, and I'm sorry for that. It's just that I had to find out more information about it."

"Well you could have called me back to let me know that everything was okay with you. How are you doing?"

"I'm not sure," I said after a brief, weird moment of silence. "Do you mind if I come and crash at your house for a while?" I asked

"At my house?"

"Yes at your house,"

"Are you sure?"

"Positive,"

"Where are you now?" Jenny asked.

"I'm at the corner of the block from my house," I answered.

"Yeah, but why are you calling me from a pay phone? Are you sure that everything is okay?" she asked.

"It's a long story. This whole day has been really hectic. I don't feel like explaining right now, and I don't feel like being at home," I explained.

"Well, you know that you are always welcome to come over here. Did you try talking to your mom about Mike?" she sincerely asked.

It really wasn't the situation with Mike that had caused me to run, even though that was part of it. It was my mother's attitude that encouraged me to leave. But I didn't want to let Jenny know that.

"Yeah, and I don't think that I can really talk to my mother right now. I need to talk to somebody I can trust."

"Well, you know I'm here when you need me. Do you remember how to get here?" she asked.

"Yep, I sure do."

"Well, come on over," she said "And don't worry about the cab fare; we will take care of that." she said.

"Thanks, Jenny. I'll be there in a few minutes then." I said.

I think that it might be time to leave my mother's house for good.

I sat in the back seat of the cab and asked a honest question:

Lord, my body is getting tired of being abused. Should I have stayed in that place?

And there was no answer.

Lord, I know that I'm not supposed to disrespect my mother. I want to love her. But how can I show her love while she's abusing me mentally, physically, and emotionally? I don't know what to do, where to go, or how to support myself out here in this world. All I ask is that if I'm wrong, let it be revealed. And if I'm right, please protect me. I'm confused, lonely, and scared, and I don't know which way to turn. I need strength to keep going. Please don't let anything happen to me or my mother.

AMEN

Chapter Six

"The supernatural camera over my head"

I arrived at Jenny's house in less than thirty minutes. Though I had five one-hundred-dollar bills stashed inside my pocket, I pretended I was strapped for cash. Even though Jennifer offered to pay the cab fare, I still planned on keeping my little $500 a secret.

I watched Jenny step out of her house and onto the front porch. I got out of the cab, patted my pockets, and shook my head. Jenny held up her index finger, turned around, and walked back into the house. Ms. Taylor came out carrying her wallet.

"Nicole, it's so good to see you. Go on inside. And don't worry, I will take care of the fare for you." Ms. Taylor welcomed me with the warmest hug.

The outside of the house was very beautiful. The first thing that caught my eye was the crystal chandelier hanging from the ceiling. It could be seen from the outside of the house through an upstairs picture-glass window. The cul-de-sac-shaped driveway was paved with cobblestones; the trees, grass, and bushes were neatly trimmed, and the flowers bloomed evenly around the entire house.

On the inside of the house, the glossy hardwood floors in the living room were very elegant. The living room was the most peaceful and cozy place to relax in the house. The living room area was filled with beautiful statues and exotic African sculptures. The furniture was of an Italian white leather plush that coordinated with the art. It accentuated the glass end tables and the Italian rug. And to make the room feel more like a million bucks, there was a black grand piano in the corner with aromatherapy candles sitting on the top.

When Jennifer took me to her huge kitchen in which the grey granite-top counters accented the high-quality, state-of-the-art, stainless steel appliances, I felt like I hit the lottery myself. The kitchen table was made of a rich burgundy cherry wood, which is the same material used to make violins and cellos.

Wow I thought, *"this is a beautiful atmosphere."*

We sat down at the table, upon which a slice of her mother's famous homemade cheesecake was sitting on the most expensive looking piece of china I had ever seen.

"Jennifer, this house feels like a dream," I said while glancing around the room

"You know what, Nicole? It is a dream. It was my mother's. It's a blessing to have all this. When mom graduated with her degree in finances, she landed a job with Daimler-Chrysler. They made her the head of the accounting department, which has an excellent salary, a great retirement plan, and good health coverage."

"Are you serious?" I said in surprise. "So lots of hard work does pay off, huh?"

"Oh yeah. Most definitely. And she worked hard, too. Then, on top of all of her accomplishments, she graduated at the top of her class. Magna cum laude," she said, taking a forkful of her pie.

"That is amazing, I remember when Ms. Taylor used to stay up all night baking and studying the Bible and her schoolbooks. I wish I knew where she gets her strength from," I said.

"No, Nick! Don't forgot that her name is not Ms. Taylor anymore. Her name is now Mrs. McArthur. You can't let her know that you forget she married the man that owns McArthur Cleaners."

"Oh yeah, that's right she did marry Mr. McAuthur. He is a good catch for her."

Jennifer took a swig of her milk and sat the cup on the table just as gently as her voice changed.

"Did you know he just opened up twenty-four more cleaner stores inside the country?"

"Twenty-four?" I asked

"Twenty-four," she repeated. "And business is doing good at those locations as well."

"I am so happy for y'all. I don't know what to say," I said as I hunched my shoulders. "And just think about it, Jenny; your mother grew up in the projects, and her mother was on drugs, right?"

"Yes, she was practically raised on welfare," she said, shaking her head up and down. Her eyes were focused on something in the air as if she was daydreaming. "It's amazing how some people grow up with nothing and end up with everything they've always dreamed of having."

Jennifer chuckled. She took another swig of her milk without losing her focus, sat the cup down, and folded her arms. "I think that he and Mom make the perfect couple."

Jennifer and I became quiet so quiet that I could hear Mrs. McArthur humming the tune "Amazing Grace" from upstairs.

"You want to know something else, Nicole?"

"Something like what?" I asked.

"I have never heard those two argue over anything," she replied before taking another bite of her pie, still in her daydreaming mode. She laid the fork on her plate and snapped back into reality. "So anyway, Nick, enough about us, I want to know about you. I know that all of this is stressful to you."

"I know it's obvious?" I asked.

"C'mon Nick; you and I have been friends for almost all our lives. I can tell what's on your mind even when you try and hide it."

"I'm okay for the most part. I will be fine. Dont worry about me."

"Look, Nicole, you had a fight at school, nearly beating the poor girl's head to a pulp. Then you got suspended from school, missing two of your midterm exams. Then Clarence's death took a toll on you. You turn around and Mike got killed. You called me and said that you couldn't talk to your mother about it, you have fresh wounds on your face, and you still won't tell me where you were when I was trying to call you."

"Call me? When did you call me?"

"When you were battling with whether leaving Mike to die was a good choice. While you were on your way home. While you were praying your soul to God, Ms. Nicole Salina Lewis!"

A spark of electricity flowed through my entire body when she said that. I noticed her staring at me like she was waiting for my revelation. I know Jennifer. She always seemed to know what was happening in my life. It's as if she had a supernatural camera placed over my head, watching over me.

"How did you know I was with Mike?" I leaned over and whispered softly.

"I called you. Your mother said you left with Mike. A few hours later, Mike dies, and you were nowhere to be found. I called you as soon as I heard about him on the news. Thirty minutes later, you pick up the phone panting and breathing hard before I could even tell you about his murder."

I wanted to cry, but feeling sorry for myself was the last thing that I wanted to do.

Jenny was right. This was a lot of stuff to deal with, and she knew it. I had so much drama in my life that I could write a novel. Maybe I could even turn it into a movie.

I pushed the saucer of pie away from me and folded my arms on the table. "Can I be honest with you, Jennifer?"

"I hope so," she answered. She got up from the table to put her saucer into the dishwasher. I waited until she washed her hands and sat back down before speaking again.

"Mom got drunk tonight. And when she gets drunk, she uses me for her personal punching bag. Things got out of hand. She hit me. I left the house."

"Is that where the big red patch on the left side of your cheek came from?" she asked, grabbing my chin, tilting my head to the right.

"Yep, this came from my mother's right hook."

"And that huge gauze pad on your forehead?" she asked, "Where did you get that from?"

"I bumped it on a cabinet." I couldn't look her in the face. If she saw my eyes, she would know that I was telling a lie.

"I thought that it was from the fight with Cocoa at first."

No, she didn't think it was from Cocoa, because the fight with her was two weeks ago. Even if it was from Cocoa, she would have known that the bruises would have been clear by now.

"You look rough, Nick. I have never seen you so scarred up like this," she said.

"Are you serious? Is it that bad?"

"Yeah, girl. Now I see where you got all your muscle from, though. You and your mother can put a dent in a Mack truck with your bare hands."

"Very funny," I said, letting out a chuckle. "You know what, Jennifer?"

"What's that, Nick?"

"I don't think I deserve it; do you?"

"Nope, I don't. That's why we allow you to stay with us until you find a solution."

Jenny got up from the table, grabbed an ice pack from her freezer, and gently placed it on my cheek. "Here, put this on it. It should take the swelling down a little."

"Feels like her fist is still in it."

"You'll be fine. Don't worry." Jenny sat down, picked up her glass of milk and finished it. "So I know you saw who killed Mike, but do the police know who did it? Did they find any clues or fingerprints?"

"The news said they had no suspects. I don't want to go to the police and tell them anything. I just want to stay low key, you know what I mean?" I asked.

Jennifer stared at me. I knew she felt sorry for me. "I hate to see you go through this, Nicole. I'm sorry about what happened to Mike. I know you really liked him."

"It's okay. I don't want you to worry about me. Mike was getting too violent, anyways. It's not like it's a big loss."

"Well, whenever you are ready to talk more about him, just know that I am here for you, okay?" She reached over and condolingly rubbed my arm.

"Okay."

We cleaned up and went outside to the pool. We took our shoes off, rolled our jeans up to our knees, put our feet in the water, and watched the stars in silence for a long time before Jennifer started talking about herself and her own personal goals.

Jennifer gave the speech about how God had blessed her with these things. She said that we serve a giving God and that all we have to do is ask for what we want and he will order our steps. He will then give us the desires of our hearts. She talked to me and encouraged me to dream big, get good grades, and make something of myself. The problem was that I had to leave her house soon. And I couldn't turn around and go home. So where would I go from here?

And there was no answer.

Chapter Seven

"Seek and ye shall find"

*J*enny and I slept peacefully throughout the night. I woke up with the sun beaming through the seated, framed window in her bedroom. If I'm not mistaken, there was a message in the sun that had been made just for me. I got up from my bed and sat down in the window where I could get a more gracious visual effect.

This is so beautiful, God. What are you trying to tell me? And the answer stood before me.

Two doves appeared in the window. They were the two prettiest doves I had ever laid eyes on. Where did they come from? I wasn't sure. However, the notion to find my father came to me.

Later on that day, Jennifer and I were in her room looking at pictures of us from when we were kids. Jenny took the faded photograph of my father from my hand and held it in the air.

"You look like your father. Especially the forehead."

"Jenny, how do you search for someone you don't know anything about?" I laid my hand on her knee as an apologetic interruption. She laid her hand on top of mine, lowered the photograph, and bumped my shoulder with hers.

"Who are you talking about? I thought you found your father," Jenny said.

"I didn't exactly find him; he came by my mother's house one day while I was at school. He gave my mother $500 for me, which I never

41

did see. And maybe it was because I was only six years old. That's the last I heard from him."

"How much personal information do you know about him?"

"I know that his name is Gregory Jerome Duncan and that he look like this picture. That's pretty much it," I said.

"We should be able to find him based on that information," she said.

"If you have the time, I sure would appreciate it if you'd help me look him up."

She bumped my shoulder again with hers. She spoke in a soothing tone. "Yeah, I got time. We can start early in the morning. Maybe try the internet first, or use the phone book to call up some numbers. Sometimes it takes a while to find someone. We'll call Maury Povich if we have to," she said.

"I don't care how long it takes, I just want to find out where he is," I said while putting the pictures back into the paper Kodak envelope. Tears formed in my eyes. "And I hope he accepts me."

"Why are you worried about how he will react?" she asked.

"I'm not really worried. I just hope he won't slam the door in my face. If he don't accept me, I'll just know that my mother was telling the truth about him all along. If he welcomes me, then I have all to gain."

"Everything is going to turn out just the way it was meant to happen, and that will be for the best of your nature. I wouldn't worry about his reaction if I were you," she said. "Once he see's how cute you are, he won't have a choice."

"Thank you Jenny." I lay back on a pillow and closed my eyes. "I wonder if he still has that afro."

Jennifer took the picture from the package and lifted it into the air. "Even if he does have that afro, you go grab a comb and brush and start doing his hair. Let that be a way to connect with him." She took me by the hand, "We'll find him. Come on Nick, let's pray that God will help us with our search."

We bowed our heads and she began to pray:

"Heavenly father, we come to you just as humble as we know how, giving you the thanks for being the gracious God that you are.

Lord, we pray that you guide our footsteps so that we may continue to be in alignment with your will. We know, Lord, that there are some things that you would rather not give to us because it is not the right time, but Lord, you also said that we don't have because we don't ask. God, we just want to ask for your hand in our search for Nicole's father. Not only that, Lord, but I also want to ask you to take ahold of Nicole's life. Show her that you are a God of mercy, strength, and power and that when she starts putting her trust in you, she will reap the benefits of everlasting life in your kingdom. Lord, we pray that in your merited favor, you will touch Nicole's father and allow him to accept Nicole with open arms as you did with us. These things I ask for in the name of your son, Jesus Christ. Regardless of your decision, we will continue to give your name the honor and glory that you so richly deserve.

We thank you for the blessing that you have given unto us. Amen!

After a brief moment of silence, she asked, "Feeling better?"

"Yeah, I do feel better."

We spent the next several months trying to locate my father. We spent hours searching on the Internet, in the yellow pages, and in newspapers, and we still could not find him. I grew tired and weary, but Jenny insisted that we keep looking. She had faith when I wanted to call it quits.

"I'm going to make a couple more calls and call it quits," I said to Jennifer.

"Well, while you're doing that, I need to wash my underarms." She raised and sniffed each arm, her mouth turned upside down. "These armpits of mine are causing havoc to the air."

"Yeah, I know. So are mine. Try not to use all the hot water." As she walked out the door, I picked up the phone and dialed the next number on the list.

If this next person isn't my real father, Lord, I hope he can volunteer to be one, I said to myself after taking a deep breath and dialing the number.

"E-yell-o."

"Hello. I am searching for a Gregory Duncan."

"This is he," He said. He sounded almost as surprised to hear my voice as I was to hear his. "Who is this?"

"My name is Nicole Salina Lewis. Do you by any chance know a lady named—"

"Nicole Salina Lewis?" he said with passion, cutting my words off.

"Yes, Nicole Salina Lewis." I concurred.

"Oh honey, I'm your father. Mm-mm-mm, I was waiting for the day when Isis would allow you to talk to me."

"Daddy?" My hand slapped against my open mouth. "Oh my God, is this really you?"

"Yeah, baby girl, it's me. You don't know how good it feels to hear your voice. I think Isis don' found her senses." he said.

"No she didn't," I answered.

"You mean she still hasn't come to her senses yet?" he politely asked.

"I meant no, she didn't give me the number. I didn't even know she had it."

"Well, of course she does. I saw her a few weeks ago and I asked about you. She told me to kiss her ass. I gave her my number anyhow, told her to call me if my child needed anything."

"Ain't that a bi---, she never told me that."

"Of course she wouldn't; she wouldn't be Isis if she did."

"Well anyway my friend Jenny and I have been searching all week for you. I was a little nervous about this whole thing," I said to him.

"There's nothing to be nervous about; I'm just glad to hear from you." he said with sincerity. He sounded like a kind and gentle man to me.

"I just thought that…well…you might not have wanted to talk to me," I said.

"Who told you that?" he asked.

"Well—"

"It doesn't matter now. Now you get to see if most of them are true," he said

"Well, why would mama try to keep me from you?" I humbly asked.

"Long story. Your mother and I couldn't agree on anything. It became too much of a battle with the courts and with her new boyfriend Harold. That's why I lay low. I did it to keep the chaos down. But I always thought about you, Nicole. You go through my mind all the time," he sincerely explained.

I wonder if Isis had been making up all these lies about my father not wanting me. I had been talking to my father for two minutes, and I love him.

Jennifer came into the bedroom and walked straight to her closet. "I forgot to grab my body wash. You should smell this new stuff I bought from this store in the—" She looked at me and froze. Her eyes looked like saucer plates with sunny-side eggs in them. "Is that him?"

"This is him," I whispered as she sat on the bed and took my hand into hers.

"Thank you, Jesus." She threw her arms up like she did in church services. "Hallelujah!"

"Who was that, honey?" my father asked as he laughed out his words.

"Oh, that's my friend Jenny. She's the one that's been helping me look for you." I answered.

"Well, tell her I said hello," he indicated.

"Well, I know I am ready to see you if that's okay with you. I've been trying to figure out where I got my good looks from. I got a picture of you from back in the seventies."

"Oh yeah?"

"Yeah."

"And which picture is that?"

"It's the one where you are standing in a driveway with a friend. You and him were leaning against a light green Ford Mustang. Your hair is in an afro, and you have on some tight khaki pants," I answered. "Dad, can I ask you a question?"

"You can ask me anything you want to."

"Have you cut your hair since then?"

"I don't have that afro anymore, darling. I think I know what picture you are talking about." He cleared his throat. "Do you see a baby blanket in the back window of the car?"

I looked more closely at the picture. There was a light pink blanket in the back window with my name embroidered on it. "Yes. I sure do. Is that mine?"

"It sure is. That was the day you came home from the hospital."

My heart dropped and my soul just opened another door.

Chapter Eight

"Isis"

The telephone rang as Isis was adding more ingredients into her pasta sauce. She tossed the enormous spoon onto the counter, splashing sauce everywhere.

"I hope this is Harold." she thought as she picked up the phone, "Hello."

"Hello. You have a collect call from the Jackson Correctional Facility. Will you accept the charges?" asked the operator.

"Yes, I'll accept the charges."

"You are now being connected. Thank you."

As the clicking began, Isis switched the phone from one ear to another and waited anxiously for Harold's voice.

"Isis? You there?" Harold asked.

"Yeah, sweetheart, I'm here. How is everything going?"

"What do you mean 'how is everything going?' I'm ready to get up out this place. How do you move your mouth to ask such a dumb question?"

Isis said nothing. She took in a deep breath through her nose and released it through her mouth. "What time are you going to be released tomorrow?"

"I told you already. You act like you can't hear sometimes. I'm getting out of here tomorrow at noon. And you better not be late this time. You remember what happened last time you were late?"

"Yeah, I remember," Isis answered. "I still got the scar on my forehead to remind me."

Harold cleared his throat. "So…uh…did you do what I told you to do, or is Nicole still in the house?"

"She's gone. I don't know where she went, though. I just hope she's okay."

"To hell with her, Isis. You did what you had to do. She stood in your face and lied. I can't believe she actually told you that I tried to rape her. She don't want to see us together. You know I wouldn't put my hands on her like she said I did. She is a liar and she is spoiled. If Nicole can't appreciate all the things you did for her, then she'll have to do things on her own." Harold leaned back against the jail wall. "So don't worry about her."

Isis leaned against the kitchen wall. She couldn't help but think about times when Harold and Nicole argued. Isis noticed something bad about Harold other than his attitude—that all of his kids are afraid of him and won't have anything to do with him.

"Isis, are you there?" Harold asked.

"Yeah, I'm still here."

"Well, say something then. You make me think you got somebody over there with you all up in your face. I will take yo' neck and—"

"There's no one here but me, Harold. Calm down. I'm here by myself. I was just listening to what you were saying, that's all."

"Yeah, okay, that's what you telling me. But I will find out what you really be doing when I'm in the pen," he said. "What were you doing when I called?"

"Cooking," she answered nervously. "And I think I should go check on it before it burns."

"Yeah, you go do that. Just be here on time and I won't go upside yo' head again. Is that understood?"

"It's understood Harold."

Chapter Nine

"…and the door shall be open unto you."

"Yes, can I help you?"

I froze as if I heard a hungry pit bull growling. I have been standing here staring at Gregory's door for five minutes without knocking. I was scared as hell when he jerked the door open. I almost swung on him.

"Did you need something?" he repeated

"Hi I'm umuh I'm Nicole, your daughter." I extended my palms out for a handshake, but he rejected it.

"Well you don't have to stand at the door like a lost dog, come on in"

My thought was, *I am a lost dog. That's why I'm here.*

"Po' thangs nerves all screwed up," He said before shaking his head and closing the door behind me. He finally extended his arms out and gave me the tightest hug. I was hoping the hug wouldn't end for at least another hour. "Are you okay?"

"Oh, yeah. I'm fine now," I answered.

His house was a mess. Ashtrays overflowed with cigarettes. Newspapers were stacked against an old reclining chair. Dust layers were on the shelves. There was a jelly filled KFC biscuit on top of the television. There were toenail clippings on the coffee table. This was not to mention the raggedy old *Sanford-and-Son* junk truck parked in the driveway.

Now wait a minute, I can understand the toenail clippings, but how did the jelly biscuit end up on the television?

"Excuse the gas smell, baby girl. I was trying to carry the can outside to the lawnmower and wasted some of it on the carpet."

"Oh, it's fine. I can hardly smell a thing."

Okay. So what. I lied. This is one of those cases where you either tuck a lie in and be welcomed to stay or tell the truth and get kicked out.

"Won't you have a seat?" he said. He cleaned a spot from the couch and gestured that I sit there.

"Thanks," I said, double checking for any debris that may cause harm to my clothes or my skin.

While putting my bags on the floor and sitting in the chair, I was able to get a good look at my father. He is a handsome old man. My eyes look like his, my nose is a carbon copy, and his forehead explains the reason kids used to tease me. So now I know who's fault it is that my nickname was "Big screen TV."

"What happened to your forehead?" he asked.

I had taken the bandages off while I was over at Jennifer's. The rock that had hit my forehead during Mike's murder left a nasty scar on my forehead. To me, it's just a permanent tattoo.

"I bumped my forehead on a cabinet. It's nothing," I said to him instead. It was too early to talk about Mike to him.

"Looks like it was a deep cut, too," he said. As the quiet breeze blew softly through the window, he sat up in his chair and scanned the scar. Hunching his shoulders, he leaned back and scanned around the room with his eyes. "I guess you are probably wondering why I didn't clean up the place before you came."

"Not really."

He cleared his throat, "Even though we've been talking on the phone for the past three weeks, we never could get deep into a conversation where we would tell all. So tell me what kind of things you like to do in your spare time, what your favorite movie is, you know, things like that."

"I don't know where to begin." I said to him as I twiddled my fingers.

"Well, first things first. You did say you got kicked out of school, right?" he asked as he grabbed the pack of Newports from the table. He leaned over and offered me one, but I refused.

"No thanks, I don't smoke."

"That's good. Go ahead with your answer," he suggested.

"Well, I've missed a lot of school days. I have to take up French and government in summer school in order to graduate."

"How did you miss a lot of days of school?" he asked.

"Well, Mom and I get into arguments all the time. Either I have to leave the house and stay with somebody or I have to try to rent a hotel."

"Rent a hotel?" he asked in surprise.

"Yes, rent a hotel."

"Okay, finish," he demanded while leaning back in his recliner and taking a drag of his cigarette.

"My teachers allowed me to make up some of the work, but I still wound up failing the course," I answered

"But how are your grades for the other classes?" he asked.

"Well, I really don't know yet. We haven't received our report cards. But I am confident that I passed those courses."

My hands needed to be busy. Now I wished I would have accepted a cigarette from him instead of rejecting it.

"You got a boyfriend?"

"No," I answered quickly, giving him full eye-to-eye contact. That question felt weird. It almost felt like he was going to ask about Mike. Before he got too personal, I felt the need to draw my line. "So, Gregory…do you have a woman?"

"Oh, okay. So I have the pleasure of being called Gregory now, huh?" He paused to take another drag on his cigarette, and he blew the smoke out forcefully. "I guess I deserved that, providing that I didn't pursue my visitation rights. Right?"

I sat back in the dusty sofa and inhaled softly. "I'm sorry. I'm just not sure what to call you yet. It's like I want to call you Daddy, but you haven't been around much."

"It's okay. You don't have to explain it. Hell, I feel a little uncomfortable with you calling me daddy too. Just call me whatever is comfortable for you. You can call me Father, Old G., Pops—whatever you feel comfortable doing."

"Papa G." I looked up in an awe. "Papa G sounds cute."

He paused and took a deep breath. "Then I'm cool with that too," He said, shaking his head continuously. "If you want to talk more about why I didn't fight harder to see you, then we can talk about that. We can talk about anything you want to. Whatever is comfortable for you. You dig?"

"Yep…I dig." I answered.

After a brief moment of silence and a few drags of his cigarette, he said, "Did you tell me whether or not you had a job?"

"No, we never discussed that," I said, picking up an Ebony magazine and flipping through the dusty pages. "I asked Isis if she would take me to a couple of places to fill out applications, but she grabbed her keys and told me to take a bus."

He let out a snicker. "What's wrong with the bus? We all gotta crawl before we walk."

"Everything is wrong with the bus. Some of the craziest freaks ride that city bus. Especially at night. Shoot! Afternoons is the only schedule I could work. I don't want to be at the bus stop at 12:00 a.m. in the morning. How does that look?"

"You need to carry you a handgun, then. That's what we used to do back in the day. Wasn't no fool on the bus gone scare me from making my money."

"C'mon now, Lets be realistic here."

When he finally stopped his obnoxious snickering, he threw his right hand in the air as if he was taking an oath. "Okay, okay. Let me stop it with the jokes 'cause we all know that carrying a gun is not a good idea."

"No, its not. But don't think I haven't thought about it," I said, tossing the magazine onto the coffee table. After we watched the cloud of dust rise and settle, we focused our attention back on what we were talking about.

"Lemme ask you a question, Nicole. Have you ever thought about going to college, or taking up a trade?"

"I don't know. I thought a lot about opening up a beauty salon or going to school to be a French teacher. But I don't know," I said, crossing my legs and playing with my fingernails. "Dreams like that don't happen to people like me."

"What do you mean 'like you'? Honey, don't you know that if you can vision it, you can achieve it? Let me tell you something, it ain't easy opening your own business. It takes hard work and dedication." He leaned forward in his chair. "But it sho' nuff ain't as hard as you think it is. Ya dig?"

"Yeah, but I can barely finish high school. I like doing hair, but I don't have any skills. If I'm gon' open up a shop, I need to go to school and get licensed. Which by the way—where would I stay while I go to school? I mean, I need to be looked after. You see that mom's house is off the list." While nervously waiting for him to stop my bickering, I sat back in my chair. I leaned my head back and closed my eyes, "I honestly don't know what I'm going to do with myself after high school."

"You know what? If you keep having those visions, somehow, someday, it will happen. But you'll never know until you venture out on your own and find your way." He stood up from his seat. "You hungry?"

"I'm starving."

"Can you cook like your mother can?" he asked, smiling from ear to ear.

"Hecky naw. Can you?"

"Hecky naw. I got some beans and rice left over from yesterday. You want that?"

I gave him the same distraught look I had when I first came in. "Beans and rice? That is not food. Living over there at Isis's gourmet kitchen made me used to eating good food. Can we at least order a pizza? Because you are not about to kill me with no beans and rice," I responded while laughing. "I'll even pick up the bill."

"Now how is it that a person with no job can offer to pay for a thirty dollar pizza? Can you tell your father where you get money from?" He reached into the side pocket of his chair and pulled out a stack of pizza coupons. "I'll handle this. I hope you like The Pizza Palace, because that's the only pizza I eat."

"Pizza Palace is my favorite too; I don't eat much of anything else," I replied.

"I see we share the same interests in taste," he said. "I hardly eat pizza too. But when I do, I always order from there and put thirty dollars' worth of toppings on it."

"Okay. I'm down with that," I said, smiling from ear to ear.

At least I won't starve for attention. Thank you, God, for listening to Jennifer Nyrese Taylor,because I think that this could be the beginning of a beautiful friendship between my father and me.

During dinner, Gregory talked about what he did for a living. He said he was a handyman. He claims he does plumbing, plastering, roofing, aluminum siding, and gutters, and he can lay down flooring quicker than a jackrabbit. During the whole time he was talking to me, I was looking around the room and thinking, *How can a person work for a job that builds tear down his own surroundings at the same time,?*

All the cleaning supplies I needed were easy to find. When Gregory left for a project assignment, I grabbed the mop, the dustpan, the dust rag, the vacuum, and some soap and water, and I cleaned all the sinks, the floors, the carpet, the furniture, and the walls. Finally, I washed all the rugs and took the trash out.

After my two hour shower, I sat at the dining room table and organized all of his utility bills. I sorted them by date and marked the ones that needed to be paid and put them in one pile, and put all the old ones in another pile.

I see that I will have to lay down some cleaning rules in here 'cause this don't make sense how he lives, I thought.

He was shocked to see his carpet's original color. He looked in the kitchen and saw that the grease on the stove could actually come off and that he didn't need to buy a new stove, but that he could just clean this one. He went inside the bathroom and sniffed around.

"Damn! It smell fresh in here, and it's been a long time since I seen this bathroom that clean."

He reached into his pocket, and pulled out a wad of money while his eyes stayed fixed on the clean bathtub.

"Nicole, I want you to take this two hundred dollars and treat yourself with it, okay?" he suggested, passing me ten of his twenty-dollar bills.

"Ewe-wee. Thanks G, I really needed this."

"Uh uh, honey, I needed this too." He placed his hand on my shoulder. "Now, can you go hook up that roast that's sitting in the freezer?"

Chapter Ten

"I need hammer and nails"

Over the next several months, my father and I maintained a stable relationship. There was one more week until summer classes, and I felt more confident to start school than I ever had. I had a stable roof over my head and more clothes on my back. There was nothing in the world that could make me give up now. These summer classes could be knocked out without hesitation, and the plan to graduate was in progress—at least for the most part.

Papa G and I had a long talk about my mother. He thought I should be mature about everything and give Isis a call. I tucked it in, sucked it up, and dialed the number.

Harold answered the phone. "Yeah?"

"Isis, please," I request.

"Who?"

"Isis," I repeated. "Is Isis there?"

"And who the hell is this?"

"Who the hell is this?" I asked in irritation.

"I think you know who this is."

"Would you put my mother on the phone please? Thank you!"

"She's cooking. And what took you so long to call? You can't call nobody and tell us where you are?"

Us? Did he just say *us?* What makes him think I need to check in with him? Stupid dummy.

"I don't think I owe you anything after what you did to me, you child molester."

"See. Look at that attitude. That's why yo' ass is out there and I'm in here," he said, snickering.

"Whatever, Harold. Put Isis on the phone,"

"Aight, Hold up."

After a few seconds of nerve-wracking noises and a mumbled comment, he finally passed the phone to Isis.

"Girl, what do you want? I'm busy."

"And hello to you too, Mommy Dearest," I greeted her, switching the phone from one ear to the other. "I just called you to see how you were doing and to let you know that I'm doing okay over here."

"Over here where? Are you in jail again?"

"No I am not in jail. I'm at my father's house."

"Wait a minute; did you say father's house?" she asked.

"I found Gregory, Isis."

Isis scoffed "Who in the hell told you to go and dig him up? And how did you find him, anyway?"

"It shouldn't matter. He told me that I was more than welcome to come and stay with him while I finish school. He's the one who told me to be the adult and make the first call to you."

"And that sounds like something his punk ass would say, too."

I wish I had a hammer and some nails so I could nail that unrighteous son-of-a-bitch on a wall. I can just see Harold sitting on the other side of her, instigating.

"So now you can come get the rest of your shit out of the room? I need space for the new baby," she said.

"New baby? What baby?"

"I'm three months pregnant, Nicole. You need to come over as soon as possible, clear your things out of the closets, and take them with you. I hope you don't plan on coming back."

So that was it. Just like that. Come and get your shit so I can have room for another jailbird bastard baby. Fuck him. Harold just couldn't wait for me to leave that house so he could move his no-job-havin' ass in there. It was a shame that he had my mother's mind twisted like this. He had her mind in the palm of his hand. Inside of dangerous hands.

"Just as soon as I find a truck."

"Well, for your own sake, you'd better move it fast before I decide to have a garage sale," she said

"You are only three months pregnant; It's not like you're going to have the baby tomorrow."

"Nicole, do yourself a favor and pretend like I am."

My heart felt like it had stopped beating, and it moved up to my throat. She would rather be with a man that treats her like dog shit than to be with her own flesh and blood. I don't know what I did to deserve this, but I knew I had better start pulling strength out of my ass now.

"Whatever I did to you Isis, I don't deserve this."

"Whatever," she replied. "It's too late to cry now. Harold says that if you don't come and get your stuff within the next few months, it's going out in the dumpster!"

Chapter Eleven

"NICOLE AND GREGORY"

Papa G unlocked his garage door, which had a double lock alarm system, and lifted the door with one hand. I was impressed. Inside sat a beautiful white Cadillac with tinted windows and a sunroof. The trimming around the border had been laced in gold. The spoke rims and whitewall Vogue tires gave it an old-school flavor. This vehicle was tight.

On the other side of the Cadillac was a red Dodge Ram. This truck was nice too. It was shiny, red, had four doors, twenty-inch tires, a CD changer, and a sunroof. I thought it was just right to move my stuff in until I saw him walking toward the Cadillac.

"Hey G, where are you going?"

"I'm taking you to go get your stuff from Isis's house."

"Yeah, but…in this?" I asked.

He didn't answer. He picked up a towel from the shelf and began wiping the dust from the hood of the Cadillac.

"Dang G, I ain't know you rode like this," I mumbled through my clutched teeth.

"There's a lot of things you don't know about yo' pops." After jingling his keys like Christmas bells, he finally picked out the one that unlocked the bar from his front wheels. Whoa! Locks on the wheels? I didn't know they made bar locks for the wheels. That's an anti-theft system for a playa—on the real.

"You ain't know I used to roll with Jet-Money's crazy ass back in the day either, did you?"

"Straight up?" I said out of shock. "Please tell me that y'all are still cool with one other."

"Cool with who?" His voice snapped as if I said the wrong thing. "Girl, don't you know that Jet-Money and your daddy used to do some of the most craziest shit together? We damn near ran the whole west side of this town until one day…he decided to go after a pregnant woman who owed him money."

"And then what happened?"

"Well, baby girl, let's just say that woman had too many children in her house that didn't deserve to see their mother get killed in front of them."

"Where were the children?"

"The children were standing around, watching the whole thing, holding on to each other."

"Are you serious?" I was shocked as hell, and my face balled up like a stingy man's hand.

"Yep. That's when your father woke up. I realized that I was too old for that bullshit lifestyle, and I didn't want to be a part of it anymore. Plus, your mother was pregnant with you at the time."

As he hit the key switch to deactivate the alarm system of the Cadillac and hung the lock bar for the wheels onto a utility hook, I watched my father's facial expressions. He looked like was having a bad flashback. Although I adored the rough side of his past, I was glad that he came out of his lifestyle not only for himself, but also for us. I saw the thug in him when I first saw him. All I knew was that there was no other man in this world who ever made me feel more secure than my father was making me feel right now.

"Get in." He gestured. He opened the driver's-side door and sat down.

I got into the Cadillac and closed the door.

"You like this, don't you?"

"Hell yeah," I said, rubbing my hand across the dashboard, "but are you sure you want to be moving furniture in this car?"

"Furniture? I thought you said you had some goddamn clothes and a few personal items. I don't use this baby to move furniture." He took a cigarette from the pack, lit the end, and started up the car. "You better not bring your ass outside with a damn chair. I'll whup your ass."

"I don't need a chair. All I need is my clothes, which I don't have much of." I turned around to look in the back seat. "Don't you think the trunk would be more efficient to carry everything?" I asked. "The trunk is empty right?"

"Mm-hm," he mumbled, his lips gripping the cigarette as he popped the gear into drive. He pulled the Caddy out of the driveway, hit the automatic garage door button, and pulled out.

Chapter Twelve

ISIS AND HAROLD—THE EXIT

"Isis. What in the hell is taking you so long in the bathroom? We are going to the casino, not the church," Harold explained as the unlit Newport cigarette bounced from his crusted lips. "C'mon woman, let's get going!"

"Five more minutes." Isis announced from the bathroom "That's all I need is five more minutes."

"Well, since you need some more time, how 'bout I just go down here and count my stash?" Harold said to himself as he walked down into the basement. He reached behind the water heater and pulled out a locked metal box. He placed the money from his pocket on the pool table along with the box. He pulled a chair up and begin counting.

"Two, four, six, eight, one thousand. Two, four, six, eight, two thousand. Two, four, six, eight, three thousand. Three thousand ought to be enough. I know I'm supposed to be paying Jet-Money his six thousand, but his ass will have to wait one more day."

After stashing the rest of his money into the safe metal box, he placed it behind the water heater and returned to the bathroom, where Isis was putting on some of Nicole's cherry lip gloss.

"What in the hell are you putting on your lips, woman?" Harold asked.

"Lip gloss, Harold, what does it look like?"

"Like a fuckin' kid." He pulled a Kleenex from the box. "Take it off! Now!"

"What?"

"You heard me; I said take it off now!" he shouted.

"Harold, it's just lip gloss; damn. I don't see what the problem is," She said, grabbing a Kleenex from the counter instead of taking the one from his hand. She began dabbing it.

"You are a grown woman and you wearing cherry lip balm from your daughter's make up case. Don't let me see you wearing none of Nicole's stuff again. Do you understand me?"

"Whatever, Harold."

Harold walked out of the bathroom and stood in the kitchen waiting for Isis to come out.

They turned on the house alarms, locked the door, and got inside the car.

Chapter Thirteen

NICOLE AND GREGORY-THE STAKE OUT

Gregory checked his wristwatch. "Nicole, are you sure they go to the casino every Wednesday at seven?" he asked. "We've been parked on this corner for almost an hour. My legs get stiff when I sit for too long."

"I'm positive," I answered. "Must be trying to get some money up from somewhere." I closed my eyes, took a deep breath, and blew it out effortlessly. I imagined Harold rummaging through my room, looking for anything with value to take to the pawn shop. And not to say the least, I pictured him putting his hands under my mattress. All I could do was pray that neither him nor Isis found that money.

"You know what, Pop? I heard that your boy Jet-Money is looking for Harold. Harold borrowed money from him and didn't pay him back."

"Is that right?"

He scooted further into the driver's seat and turned down the sounds of my girl Mary J. Blige's song "Take me as I am," which was playing on the radio. "So Harold owe Jet some money, huh?"

"Yeah. Big money."

"Humph."

"Harold still haven't paid him back. Harold say that he ain't paying him back shit."

"Is that right?" he asked

"Yep. And I hope Mom doesn't get caught in the crossfire when Jet-Money comes looking for him."

"You know what, Nicole? There's one thing Jet never does—hurt other people. If you aren't the one who took the money from his hands, he won't bother you. He just goes after the hand he laid the cash in. He does this so that the other people can witness who he is. And plus, Jet-Money know your mother. He might not like her too well, but he won't hurt her."

And I knew that for a fact. Jet-Money could have had me killed when he was after Mike, but he didn't. He could have killed those kids Dad was talking about, but he didn't.

I was just trying to get Harold dealt with. But it was obvious that Harold was going to be dealt with in due time.

"I just think Harold deserves the same treatment he gives to Isis, though. What right does he have putting his hand on someone?"

He thumped the ashes from the lit cigarette outside the partially rolled-down window and cleared his throat. "I could never hit your mother, but I can admit I wanted to. Your mother pushed me so many times toward that limit that I almost wanted to choke her. But instead I did the same thing you did when she hit you in the kitchen—I left." He took a long drag of his cigarette and forced it out before he continued. "You see, Nicole, it takes a real man to get up and walk out instead of hitting a female. That is what really makes a man. I can understand why you left. You wanted to hit her, but the good person in you knew that it wouldn't be a good idea."

I laid my left hand on top of his arm gently. "Thanks for understanding me, Papa G."

Isis's car backed into the street. As Harold put the car into drive and sped from the driveway, the tires blew up a cloud of smoke.

Gregory looked at me and shook his head. "That must be the dumbest mutha fu—"

"He's dumber than you think," I said, cutting into his words. After slipping my hands into my leather gloves, I opened the passenger-side door. "I'll be back."

He took a deep breath "Be careful, Nicole. Just get what you need and come right out." he insisted. Gregory took a drag of his cigarette and flicked the filter out of his driver's-side window. "I will give you about five minutes to gather things up, and then I'll pull in front of the house."

"Five minutes is all I need." After stepping out of the car and closing the passenger door, I looked around to see if anyone was watching us. Luckily, there was no one around as far as my eyes could see.

When I got to the back of the house, the next-door neighbors startled me. They were sitting in their back yard, watching their two daughters play in the sandbox. For Christ's sake, it was now eight o'clock at night; shouldn't these kids be in the bathtub and getting ready for bed?

I wasn't trying to listen to the neighbors' conversation, but I overheard them talking about us. I stooped down and hid behind Isis's favorite rose bushes. I was cool until one of the thorns snapped back and grazed the left side of my face.

"Ow! Shit!"

I wasn't worried about the pain so much; I was more concerned about blowing my cover. After checking over the bushes and realizing I hadn't been heard, I put my hand over the scarred area, checking for blood. Now not only did I have a scar from Mike's murder and redness in my face from Mom's hook, but I also had a nicely pencil-shaped cut on my other cheek. Now my face was dramatically filled with war wounds.

I brushed it off with my gloves and turned my attention back to the next-door neighbors' conversation.

"Trisha, the man who knocked on our door yesterday wanted blood. He didn't look like he was into playing games with Harold. I'm telling you the truth—something is about to happen; I can feel it," Mr. Nelson, the next-door neighbor, announced.

"Well let's just pray we don't get caught up in their mess," Mrs. Nelson replied. "You and I have been dealing with them for several years now. It's the same thing year after year. I'm 'bout tired of dealing with those crazy people next door—and their drama. I think it's about time we look into moving into another house. We can't raise kids next door to these types of people."

"Yeah, well, there's definitely something about to go down over there now baby. I think we need to just keep the kids in the house for a while."

"Yeah, I agree with you on that one," She said to Mr. Nelson before directing the kids into the house. I was finally in the clear to go inside the house and unnoticeably take care of my business.

After unlocking the door and going inside, I closed the door and turned the alarm system off. When I reached the top of the stairs, I paused in front of my old bedroom door.

"Lord, please have mercy on my mother, for she does not know what she does," I said.

As I heard the Nelsons' conversation play inside my head, I twisted the doorknob and walked inside. To my surprise, the room was filled with baby items.

"Where the—?" I yelled at my empty room. "Where is my stuff?"

I took a deep breath. Trying to stop the tears from rolling down my face, I closed the door and walked toward the attic. I was amazed at myself for trying to give Isis the benefit of the doubt in not letting Harold trash my belongings. I opened the attic door. "I hope my mother had the decency to move it up here."

To my surprise, even the attic was empty.

I went into the basement. It was the same thing—empty.

Mad as hell, I turned the burglar alarm on and walked out of the back door. This time I wasn't concerned about anyone seeing me. I didn't give a damn who saw me exiting this place.

"Where are your clothes?" my father asked as I got inside the car.

"All my stuff is gone. I couldn't see anything in that house that belonged to me. Not even a tube of lip gloss or a picture." My face fell into the palms of my hands. "They must have thrown it all out."

"Are you sure? Did you look in the basement?" Gregory asked.

"I looked in the basement and the attic, and there was nothing there," I said to him. He took a cigarette from the Newport box and lit the end. He leaned back and stared at the side of my face.

"Well, damn. Who let the cat out of the bag?" he asked.

I lifted my hands from my leather gloves. "A cat? What the heck are you talking about?"

"You don't feel that blood dripping off the side of your face? What happened to you?"

I took my gloves off and flipped the visor mirror open. "It came from that raggedy-ass rose bush in the back yard," I said to him. "I bet I got blood everywhere. I feel so stupid."

"Don't feel stupid, baby girl; just wipe it off," he said, passing me a handkerchief from his coat pocket. "You have nothing to feel stupid about. We can work on getting you some new clothes. Don't worry," he said to me as he put the vehicle into drive and pulled off slowly.

While wiping the blood from my face with the handkerchief, I wasn't worried about my clothes. I actually felt more stupid for not going back into the house the night I left. My money was in that mattress, and I was mad as hell. That money was what I really wanted. My father thought I was crying about my clothes. Fuck the clothes. I was mostly crying for the loss of the $9,500. Damn! Can't blame no one but myself.

And I asked God yet another question:

"Why me?"
And there was no answer.

Chapter Fourteen

"A new friend"

Summer finally arrived. It was now time to sign up for my two summer classes, graduate, and end all the agony of getting a high-school diploma. I tried to put the loss of the money behind me and move on, but it was tough. It was it the hardest thing I have ever done in my life. How the hell could I forgive and forget $9,500?

I spent half of the day trying to obtain my records from my old school. When I got them into my hands, I spent another hour in line trying to sign up for my French and government classes. When I finally reached the front of the line, I came across a familiar face. Her name was Mrs. Beasley. She used to work at as a lunch lady at the middle school I attended five years ago. She was nice. She would always give me a double scoop of whatever I wanted.

"Name, please."

"I'm Nicole Salina Lewis. I had my forms faxed over from another school," I answered with confidence. "And how are you today, Mrs. Beasley?"

"And why would your forms be sent here?" she asked, ignoring my question. But I continued on.

"Because I wanted to sign up for summer classes."

"Have a seat. I will check the fax machine to see if your records were sent as soon as I am done dealing with these people," she answered hastily.

The lines were as long as the lines in malls on a holiday. This is ridiculous, every time I try to make progress in my life, a force comes and sends a long line of people ahead of me, testing my patience. Finally, after an hour of waiting in the office, Mrs. Beasley waved her hand as a gesture for me to come up to the desk.

Rising from my seat, I walked up to Mrs. Beasley, who was reaching into the fax machine. She pulled out three sheets of paper and a manila folder and tossed them on the counter.

"Here is your schedule, Nicole. These are the times and days you'll be attending your classes, and these are the room numbers. When or if you graduate, your cap, gown, and a tassel will be issued to you for a senior fee of $200. You will have a graduation ceremony for your immediate family only. Your first class starts Monday. If you miss more than four days, you will be excluded from that class, you won't graduate, and you will have to take the class or classes again in the fall. Any questions?"

"No, I think I got all the answers I need."

"Good luck," she said, pushing my schedule across the desk. "Next in line, please."

Bitch.

After taking a deep breath and exhaling, I grabbed my schedule from the counter while rolling my eyes at her. I stormed out of the office door, making a vow to myself that I wasn't going to let anyone or anything stop me from graduating. Not even a snobbish staff member could break my ambition.

When I walked into the classroom on Monday morning, I spotted an empty seat in the back of the room and sat down. I picked it because the window view was facing the back yard of the school. The flowers were nicely planted, and the breeze that seeped through the window reminded me of being on the beach.

When I sat down, this thinly built girl sat next to me. She reminded me of the singer Aaliyah. She was wearing the sharpest stiletto boots that money could buy. She was ending a conversation on her cellular phone as she sat down. The class settled down just as the teacher was walking in.

"*Bonjour, classe. Je m'appelle* Mademoiselle Wittlemoore." She was a tall, thinly built woman with glasses on her nose. She floated her ass into the classroom like she was in love with a stripper.

"*Bonjour,* Mademoiselle Wittlemoore!" the class answered in unison.

"Can anyone tell me what I just said?" Ms. Wittlemoore asked.

The pretty, brown-skinned, stiletto-heeled girl who was sitting next to me looked over and replied by saying, "Hell naw."

I laughed.

Ms. Wittlemoore paused and looked at the girl, but paid little attention to her. Mademoiselle Wittlemoore focused her attention back on her class. "From now on we will speak, write, listen, and breathe French inside my classroom," Ms. Wittlemoore announced.

"But Ms. Wittlemoore," the stiletto-heeled girl said, "I can inhale and exhale this shit in all day long, I'm still not gon' get this crap."

"If you don't pass the course, you will not graduate on time. So you'll just have to do what you have to do to make a passing grade," Ms. Wittlemoore answered.

The girl fanned her hand toward the teacher and popped her teeth. She pushed her notebook to the side and laid her head on the top of her desk. "Forget this dumb class. I hate French."

Ms. Wittlemoore showed the girl no regard. She turned around and grabbed the chalk from the chalk plate. She began writing the lesson on the chalkboard.

Taking a sheet of paper from my binder, I began writing the girl a letter:

> *"Hello, my name is Nicole. I know that you don't know me from a can of paint, but I can help you get through this. I love French. The only reason I have to take this class over is because of things that happened in my personal life. I can help you pass this class if you need it. The opportunity is here, but it's up to you to take advantage of it. Just do what you can and I will help you with the rest.* ☺ "

I folded the letter and passed it to her.

"What's this?" she asked with a frown on her face.

I flashed her a warm smile. "Just read it; it's okay."

She hunched her shoulders, took the letter from my hand, and opened it. She read it, folded it up back up, and tucked it inside her folder. She looked at me and smiled as if I were Jesus himself and nodded her head.

"Name's Chrystal," she said. "Nice to meet you, Nicole."

"Same here," I said.

Chrystal took out a pink notebook and began copying the lessons that Mrs. Wittlemoore was writing on the board.

I watched her as she shook her head in shame throughout the class but kept her endurance. I laughed with her and flashed a smile or two in between the lectures. "You gon' be okay; I got your back," I told her. I saw that the more I assured her, the more she found herself pressing on a little further.

When the class was over, I packed up my notes, turned in my class work, and went outside.

"Where in the heck is my father? I thought I told Gregory what time the class ended."

While waiting for his arrival, I made myself a spot on the grass by the end of the fence and sat down. The parking lot was full of people driving away in their own vehicles. I became jealous.

"I could have had a car if only I'd turned around and got my money from that mattress." I said to myself. Several times I had tried to forget about it, but that was hard. The only time I really hate myself is when I don't have the money to get what I need.

Hitching a ride from parents is bullshit. Especially at this age. I hope he pull up in the Cadillac or the Ram. I hope he don't embarrass me with that old broken down Sanford and Son truck of his.

As I glanced behind me at the exit door, the stiletto-heeled girl from French class walked out. The crowd around her painted a picture of her popularity as they walked up to her like she was a goddess. It was a picture that I might not be in the position to hang on my wall yet.

She probably has friends that she can pay to do her homework. I thought to myself. She had the fellas stopping and flirting with her. She was dressed in expensive clothes and her hair wasn't out of place at all. She carried herself with a lot more confidence than I ever will.

"What makes me think she needs my help, or that she wants my help for that matter?" I asked myself. Turning around to mind my own business, I pulled a French note from my notebook.

"Hey, Nicole." She walked up from behind and tapped me on the shoulder.

I stood up as though she was the queen of England. Now all of a sudden I saw how popular she was, and I became shy. "Ohhello."

"I had to come over and thank you for what you said to me in the classroom," she said as the scent from her expensive perfume slid my way.

"What did I say?" I curiously asked.

"Well, you told me that you would have my back. I appreciate that."

"Oh, yeah; I did, didn't I? Well, it's no big deal. I mean, French comes easy to me."

"*Je m'appelle* Christyl. However, my friends call me Chris," she said, extending her hand for a handshake.

"It's Nicole, but my friends call me Nick. Nice to meet you," I said, accepting her handshake invitation.

Up close, Christyl was a very pretty person. I saw why she was popular with the fellas. She had long, silky, dark, shoulder-length hair with gold highlights. She had a golden caramel-brown complexion with a pimple. She measured about the same body weight as mine, with a thinner build in the stomach area. The shirt she was wearing had a cut to show her small waist and her belly ring. Her hair, toes, and fingernails looked like she just stepped out of a salon, even though the wind was blowing. Her jewelry and accessories were neatly organized and coordinated perfectly with her attire.

"You don't look familiar. Are you just going here for summer school?" she asked politely.

"Yeah. I just moved on this side of town with my dad. Hopefully, I'll be finishing up my senior year at this school. I only need these two classes," I answered.

"That's cool; you're a senior too."

"Yep."

"So these are the only classes you have to take in order to graduate?" she asked.

"Uh-huh. I have to pass French and government or I'll be here in the fall doing the same shit all over again."

"Straight up? Me too. I'm glad you know what you are doing."

"I like French. It just sounds so romantic, ya know?" I told her, shifting from one leg to another.

"Pff! I dunno 'bout all that. It sounds like a whole bunch a jibber jabber. I want to understand just enough to get me through this class," Chrystal said. Both of us laughed. "I ain't trying to go to France anyway."

Shifting from a playful attitude to a more serious one, I said, "Well, this jibber jabber has to be learned before we graduate whether we like it or not."

She smiled as she opened her Prada purse. She took out a palm pilot, flipped it open, and took out a pen. "What's your number?"

"Oh, it's 313-555-6244" I said. I wanted her number too, but I was not sure how to ask for it.

"Well, don't you want mine?" she asked.

"Oh, yeahright." I took out my French notebook and a pen. "Okay, I'm ready."

"No you're not. Please tell me that you are not about to write down my phone number on your French notebook."

"What's wrong with the notebook?"

Chrystal snickered. "Do you know how many people ask for my number? If someone sees it in your notebook, it will be written all over the bathroom walls. Freshmen will be calling me."

She reached inside her leather Fendi purse again.

"Here, take this," she said. This time she pulled out a pink phonebook with angels embossed on the cover. It was still in its original wrapper. "You can have it if you want it. One of my mother's clients gave it to me as a gift. Since you just moved here and you obviously don't have a place to put your new numbers, you can have this."

I gently took it from her hands and observed it "That's real nice of you Chrystal, thank you," I said.

"Remember, it's Chris," she said.

"Oh, yeah—Chris," I said with a smile.

"Let the angels watch over you while you are here," she added. Since the brief moment of silence felt awkward, I felt the need to offer her something in return. "If you need a ride, my dad should be here any minute."

"Naw, I'm good." She took a wad of keys from her purse and deactivated the alarm to a brand-new Jeep Cherokee.

"Do *you* need a ride?" she asked.

"Oh, I'm okay, Chris. My dad is supposed to pick me up. I guess he will be here in a minute. You know how men are," I said with embarrassment.

"Yeah," she said, shaking her head up and down in shame. She turned around to walk toward the truck and waved. "See ya, Nick."

"Okay," I sung out in two different keynotes

I watched Chris get into her Jeep, start the engine, and drive away. Shortly after that, my father turned the corner in his raggedy work truck. I could hear the theme song to *Sanford and Son* going through my head.

Da-da-da-da-na

Da-da-da-da-na-da-na-dun

Da-da-da-na

Dun-na-dun-na-da-na-dun

"Hey, Sanford." I hopped into the truck and closed the door.

"Hey Son," My father replied, flashing a big smile. I leaned back in the chair as he pulled out of the parking lot. I was glad to be the last one to leave.

Chapter Fifteen

"It's too hot in this room."

"What you doing sitting up in this hot house for? Go on out there on the back porch and get some air." He took a bottle of water out of the refrigerator, opened it, and took a swig.

"I'm cool, Pops. I'm almost done anyway," I told him.

I can't lie to you. Today is hot. I could have sworn I saw Satan's ugly ass walking up and down the street this morning trying to scorch the road. If anything needed to be done in this house, it would be to get some ventilation going. And above all things, the sun felt as though it was sitting on top of the roof.

"I stopped at a hardware store to pick up some tools for that air conditioner. Two summers went by and I still haven't had a chance to fix that air conditioner. All it needed was a thermostat."

"Well, thank God. A thermostat shouldn't be to much trouble, right?"

"You're right," He reached over at the book I was studying in and flipped it to the cover. "What you got there?"

"French."

"That's right; you did tell me you had to take up a French class. Did I tell you French was one of my favorite subjects in school too?"

"Naw, you didn't tell me that," I replied. I closed the French book and slid it back inside of my bag. "The first time I heard French, I knew that one day I would visit France, hopefully live there."

"Oh yeah?"

"Uh-huh." I closed the strap on my bag and dropped it onto the floor. "I always dreamed of going to school in France too."

"That's good. Whenever you plan to go to France, get me a ticket. I want to go too."

"Cool." After a brief moment of silence, I said, "I still have problems with the masculine and feminine parts of French, but I'm getting better at it."

"My only problem is that I'm good at speaking it, but I can't understand it when I hear it," he said as he took another swig of his water. He leaned back against the wall and wiped the sweat from his forehead.

"That's a balance."

"What's a balance?" he asked.

"Us."

"What do you mean?" he asked.

"Well, I'm not good at speaking it, but I can understand it. You are good at speaking it, but you don't understand it. I think we could make a good team while we are in France."

"Sounds like a deal. Just let me know when you're ready to go to," he said as he picked up an old slice of cake that was still in its container and smelled it. His face frowned at the sight of the wretched hair growing from the icing before tossing it into the trash.

I went into my room and closed the door. I took out an old map of France that I copied from Mademoiselle Wittlemoore's class and looked it over. I cleaned up my room, folded my laundry, and vacuumed the carpet in my room. After that, I became bored.

While picking up the phone, I wondered what Chris was doing and if she felt like conversing. Even though Chris didn't seem like the type that enjoyed sitting on the phone and chit-chatting with a female, I decided to call her anyway.

I picked up the phone and dialed her number, but her phone went straight to voicemail. Oh well, so much for that plan.

The noise from the kitchen had me curious. When I walked in, Papa G's body was lying stiff underneath the sink.

"Pop? You okay under there?" I had to ask. He wasn't moving, and I was starting to think he croaked.

"Papa G? Papa Gee-ee? Are you okay?"

"Oh yeah…I'm cool. I was just trying to see what the heck is stuck inside this pipe," he answered.

"What's wrong with the sink?" I asked.

"It looked like something was in it, causing it to leak." His voice echoed up from under the cabinet. I stood across the room, watching him take one tool after another. After doing that five times, he broke the silence.

"You want to know something?" he asked. "It's a good thing that you are here. It's motivating me to fix up the place a little more. I can't have my daughter living in a house like this. You have been cleaning up for me since the first day you moved in. Bless yo' heart."

All I could do was smile. I noticed that too. Since I've been here, Papa G has been fixing up things, getting rid of things he didn't use, and paying more attention to himself for that matter. He even dresses better and use cologne. Through it all, I can say that living with my father has become a blessing to him and me both.

"Have you talked to your mother yet?" he asked.

"Nope."

"Well, don't you think you ought to call her and find out what she did with your clothes?"

"Nope," I repeated.

He slid out from underneath the sink, staring at me. "Why not?"

"I don't know, I just don't care about that stuff anymore. Plus, why should I call her when she's the one in the wrong?" I asked.

"I don't know. But at least call her and let her know you came by to get it but couldn't find it."

Call her? Call her for what? She threw all my stuff away. They put me out into the street, stole my money and he thinks I should call her? Yeah right!

"Nick, listen to me. One of you must be the mature one. Plus, you can't let her do something like that and not know the true reason she did it—unless you know already."

"Oh, I know why she did it! It was that Harold that made her do it." I said furiously.

"Harold, huh?" he asked as he grabbed another tool from the floor and slid under the counter. "Do you think he really had something to do with this?"

"I know for sure he had something to do with it."

"Tell me this Nicole, has he ever tried to give you an ass whoopin'?"

I smacked my teeth at the thought of having to go back down memory lane. "It's just that every time he gets out of jail, he ends up staying with us. She lets Harold run all over her and our house. He's probably the one who stole my money," I said to him. I felt a crying session coming on, so I grabbed a clean paper towel off the counter just in case.

"So he stole money from you?" he asked as he continued tapping on a pipe.

"He sure did, and Isis probably don't even know it."

"Mm-mm-mm. How much did he take? What…$100…$200?" he asked.

"More like $10,000."

Dad scooted up from the sink and dropped the tool. It landed on the floor in a loud thud. He jumped to his feet like Jackie Chan does in his movies and walked over toward me. He looked into my eye like he was trying to read my soul. "Did you just say he took $10,000 from you?"

"Yep," I answered.

"That's a whole lot of money, baby girl. Where on earth did you get that kind of money from?"

I remained silent. I didn't want to lie to him, nor did I want to tell him the truth. I didn't want to bring up Mike's name at all in this house.

"He did something else to me too, but…um…I don't know if it's a good idea to…uh…tell you."

"Well of course it is, sweetheart. You know you can tell me anything. I told you, you can talk to me with just about anything."

"Promise you won't do anything drastic?"

"I promise you hon. Just tell me."

"Well, he made me have sex with him. That bastard raped me." My heart dropped from my chest to my stomach. I knew I could trust my father; I hoped I could. He was the first person besides my mother who knew.

"What!" He shouted.

"It's true. I mean, it happened when I was twelve while Isis was working. He knew Isis would'nt come home within the next three hours. I came home from school, went into my room to change out of my uniform, and there he was, standing at the door, watching me, licking his old crusted lips. Then that's when he…when he…just…he just…"

Papa G stood in the middle of the kitchen shaking his head. He tried to say something, but it didn't come out. So I continued.

"I was kicking and screaming all over the place trying and get this man off of me, but I was to weak,"

"So have you told anyone else besides me?"

"Nope. Only because he told me that if I ever told anyone, he would have me killed. He also told me that I would be wasting my time telling her, because she wouldn't believe me anyway," I explained, now in full-fledged tears.

"But you told Isis anyway, right?"

"I ended up telling her what happened. She came up with the concept that I was making this all up just to get Harold out of her life."

Papa G took a seat at the kitchen table, placed his hands on his forehead, and continued shaking his head. He stared at the phone on the table and then stared out the window. Grabbing a towel, he wiped his hands and dropped it onto the kitchen floor. Finally, he reached over, took the phone from its hook, stared at the numbers on the phone piece, then put the phone back on the hook. He was confused.

"Don't worry about it honey. You ain't got to worry about him no mo'. I promise you I will take care of him myself."

I stood there crying and biting my nails. Now I was nervous.

"Pop, I don't want you to get hurt. Harold is a dangerous man."

"Dangerous my ass. Do you really think I'm scared of his punk ass?" He jumped from his seat and paced the floor. "I'm going to kick his ass."

"But Pop—"

"Fuck that. What kind of man would do this to a helpless five year old?"

"I was twelve, Pop and—"

"It doesn't matter what age you was. You were a minor!"

"I guess I should have called the police or told my teachers. I was just too afraid that he was actually going to kill me or hurt Mom," I mentioned.

"You don't have to worry about Harold bothering you anymore, baby girl. I've been looking for a reason to kick his ass. He don't know who he messed with. He just don't know that I know some people who wou—" He stopped, inhaled through his nose, and blew out through his mouth forcefully. "You just finish school and get your good grades back, all right? And let me do the rest."

"What do you mean you know some people? I don't want you getting hurt," I said. "I need you."

"You don't have to worry 'bout me getting hurt. I'm not gon' touch his ass."

I hugged my father as tightly as a Pamper on a three year old, releasing all the pain and hurt I had through my tears. I wasn't sure what he would do to Harold, but I didn't care. All I knew was that I felt protected right there in his arms and that I wanted to stay there for the rest of my life. Out of all the times I prayed that he would come, this was definitely an *in the-nick-of-time* moment.

Chapter Sixteen

"This Ain't Working"

*L*iving with a man has its advantages and disadvantages.

- <u>The advantage of staying with my father:</u> I get to drive his Cadillac, pay no rent, buy no food, come and go as I please—the basic all-American woman's dream and freedom without giving up my goodies.

- <u>The disadvantage of living with my father:</u> I have to come home from school to a dirty house. I get to smell smoke all the time. I am continuously passing out drinks to him and his friends. I cook and clean up behind them. I have to deal with the spirits behind the smoking and the drinking. And last, but not least, I always have to tell him where I'm going and when I'll be back when I'm driving his car.

One warm Saturday evening, I walked in. Pop and his two friends were sitting in the living room, drinking and smoking as usual. But this time, the smoke from the cigarettes, marijuana, and cigars was so thick that it made a big cloud in the room. Beer bottles were everywhere, and the ashtrays were full of filters and tails. On a normal day, I would come in and start cleaning. But today I made a vow to leave everything like it was, go straight to my room, and shut myself out—away from them and the world. But my plan failed. I could hear Pop yelling my name before I could get even my key in the lock to unlock the front door. I knew he was drunk.

"Nick! Nick! C'mere, baby girl. I want you to meet somebody," he demanded. I walked into the house and shut the door behind me.

"This is Phillip and that's Tony," He said, pointing at them as he called out their names. "And this is my baby girl, Nicole."

"Hi Phillip. Hi Tony. Nice to meet you both," I said, and I waved my hands.

"Aye, baby girl, Phillip was just telling me he knew somebody else who was raped by Harold."

My heart, my mouth, and my books dropped to the floor. Now why was my father going around exploiting my business to his friends? Now I was embarrassed.

"Pop, c'mon nah…you wasn't suppose to s—"

"I know what I said. I told you not to worry about it. Didn't I say that?"

I took a deep breath and forced it out. "Yeah, but you also said you wasn't going to make a big deal of this. You promised."

"I haven't promised you anything. I told you to let me handle that bastard. And I meant what I said."

Damn. My father's new personality is frightening. I guess this is just his old personality coming to the surface. Makes me wonder if I brung these demons back to him.

"Well, Tony, Phillip—again, it was nice meeting you both." I rolled my eyes at Papa G, flashed a fake smile to Tony and Phillip, and walked to my room.

"Oh, Nick? I almost forgot to tell you that Christyl called for you. She said to call her cell phone when you get a chance," he said. "You need a cell phone."

"No shit," I mumbled. I'm sick of hearing people tell me that.

Chris called with good timing. I needed to get away from this place, but I didn't want to use his car to do it. I needed to go somewhere, let my hair down, smoke a blunt maybe, and relax.

I feel happy when Chris calls. Chris is my dawg. When you see Chris, you see me. We tell each other everything now, and we share all kinds of secrets. Even when we are not in school, we still hang out together. I pick her up in Papa G's Cadillac, and we go anywhere our spirits take us. And sometimes she comes and gets me in her truck and we ride to the movies or to the mall. I'm glad I met someone who has a heart like hers.

I picked up the phone and dialed Chris's cellular number. She picked the phone up on the first ring like it was an emergency and I was here to save her life.

"You have got to get you a cell phone, Nicole."

"I know. That's the same sermon everyone has been preaching to me lately."

"Well it's true," she said. "And where have you been all this time? I have been trying to call you to see if you wanted to go out tonight."

"I just walked in, Chris. I was at the library trying to finish my research paper for the government class," I told her.

"Is that where you been all day?"

"For the most part." I took a deep breath and blew it out forcefully. "I'm open to do anything right now. I can't stay in this house any longer. I actually want to move out of here."

"Dang Nick, what's gotten into you? Papa G must be getting on your nerves again."

"Yes he is. Can you believe he just told his friends about what Harold did to me."

"Oh, no he didn't," she replied. "Why did he do that? I thought he promised not to tell anyone?"

"He did. And it's scary, because I have never seen this side of my father before. I think him and his friends are about to do something to Harold." I walked to my bedroom door just to make sure he wasn't listening to my conversation. "I'm telling you, Chris, I have got to move soon."

"Well, I can't help you move out right now. But I can come and get you out of the house," Chris said.

"And go where? I don't have any money, I don't have anything clean to wear, and my hair look like shit." I stepped in front of the mirror and frowned at the sight of my dry and flaky scalp.

"You remember me telling you about my future husband Kenny, right?"

"Kenny?" I asked.

"Yes, Kenny…the one that goes to college?"

"Yeah, I remember. What about him?"

"Well him and his friends are throwing a party tonight. It's only about an hour's drive from here. Wanna go?"

"An hour? Well where the heck is it at, Ohio?"

"Yeah…sort of." she answered.

"What time is the party?" I asked.

"Well, if you want to go, the answer is *now*. This would be your chance to see another part of the country, relax your mind, and meet some *real* men. You should go with me if you're not doing anything."

"College men? That sounds good and all, but you know I don't have anything decent to wear, and I doubt it if Dad'll let us use his Cadillac tonight."

"Forget him," she said, smacking her teeth. "I can come and get you. Momma can fit you in and do your hair. And like always, we can look in my closet and pull out something decent for you to wear that is actually not pink."

"I'm game. What time will you be here?"

"In less than thirty minutes. Right now I'm at the mall. I'll call Momma and tell her that you need touching up."

"Aight. I'll be ready in a few minutes," She said.

I showered, shaved my underarms, waxed my legs and threw on a half decent sweatshirt and pants. By the time I was done, Chris was pulling into the driveway. She was yapping away on her cell phone as usual. Talk about timing, Chris was in the nick of it.

I grabbed my house keys and my mini Coach pouch and locked the door without saying goodbye. They were too busy passing a blunt to care about me anyway. So fuck 'em.

We pulled up to Chris's house. Mrs. Manning's boyfriend, Richard, waved and winked. He was pulling his shiny, red Mercedes out of the driveway. That was weird. Richard had never winked at us before.

Just about everything that was in her house had a decor of leopard and tiger prints. The smell of shampoo and flowers filled the air every time we walked into the house. In the basement was Ms. Manning's beauty salon. That was where she worked her infinite styling skills.

"Mom, Are you ready to do Nicole's hair right now? If not, we can go up and try on some clothes."

Darlene took the iron curlers out of her customer's hair and put them in the cast iron stove. She reached over and rubbed my hair. "You just washed it didn't you?"

"Um, yeah. I didn't really need a perm."

" That's okay. Y'all can go on upstairs and get your clothes together while I finish curling CheVaughn's hair. Just give me fifteen minutes."

Chris's mother, Darlene, was a beautiful person inside and out. She had long, thick eyelashes with big, pretty, hazel eyes to match. Her beautiful and flawless caramel complexion made her look like she had make up on even when she didn't. Her waistline was as small as Chris's. And her country accent gave a stylish flavor to her attitude. She looked like she could be a stunt double for Vanessa Williams.

"Thanks for squeezing me in, Ms. Manning."

"I have told you over and over again, Nicole—call me Darlene," she insisted. "Just figure out how you want your hair and I will take care of it for you. Um-kay?

"Okay," I answered, looking up at her hair. "I like your hair color. It's beautiful. I'd like something like that."

"I could try to come as close to it as I can, even though this here is my natural color."

"Well I love it. I wish I had the same color in my hair," I said.

Darlene turned toward Chris and pointed her finger toward the stairs. "Twinkie, Why don't you take her upstairs and find her something to wear while I finish up with this customer. I'll let y'all know when I'm done," Darlene insisted.

"Aight. No problem," Chris said as she placed one foot on the steps and then waved her hand as a gesture to follow her. "C'mon Nick."

"Thanks again, Darlene." I turned to her and said, "I hope I'm not putting you through any trouble or anything."

"Oh, no. Don't worry about it. I'm almost finished with this client anyway. I got time left before the next customer comes in," she said, flashing me another one of her genuine smiles. "Plus, all you need is a blow dry and some curls. You don't have time for color. You did me a favor when you washed it."

Chris's room was huge compared to mine. It was cleaner and far too organized from top to bottom for me. But I like being in her room, except for one problem—everything in her room is pink. She has a pink ceiling fan that spins around pink feathers, a pink couch with rhinestones and jewels dangling from the lining of the couch cover, and a stuffed pink panther doll sitting on her pink comforter. And just like the other rooms in the house, she had an aquarium. The only difference was that Chris's fish tank had pink rocks layering the bottom. Go figure.

"Now look, Nicole, I think brown or gold would look nice with your complexion." She took out a beige colored halter top with glittered shingles around the breasts' lining and a pair of boys' denim jeans with boot-cut legs. "Do you like this?"

"That's tight," I answered. I stepped into her closet. "I'm surprised your closet isn't full of pink clothes."

"Mostly everything I used to wear was pink. I stopped wearing all that pink when I was around fourteen. Wearing pink all the time became kiddish and played out."

"Not really though, I see women wearing pink all the time," I said to her as I flipped through her dresses.

"A grown ass woman still wearing pink all the time? Yeah right," she scoffed as she reached into her closet. "You do like halter tops, don't you?"

"Hell yeah. Now that one is tight. I can rock this shirt with the boots I got on."

"Nuh-uh, Nick. Unless you want to look like a cheap hooker, you go ahead. She reached into her closet and pulled out a pair of boots with a silver bracelet hanging from the high stiletto heel. There were three different shades of brown in it. I must admit, this girl had excellent taste in clothes. "Here, try everything on, so that we can see how it looks."

"Can I get a little privacy please? I wouldn't want to put my big butt all in yo' face or anything," I said to her.

"Heffa, please. Nobody want yo' ass."

She took her cell phone from her pocket and flipped it open.

"I gotta call my future hubby anyway and let him know where we are. So see you in a minute."

"Bet."

I tried on the shirt first, then the pants. This looked nice. Finally, I slipped my feet into the pencil-heeled boots. Damn, my booty always look good in her clothes.

I modeled in her vanity mirror until she stepped back into the room. "Okay, lemme see it. Turn around." She brushed the lint from my shoulders, tugged on my shirt, and wiped my jeans one time. "All you need now is a good hairdo and some accessories, and you tight. I think I saw that client leave, so she must be ready for you."

"Okay, give me a minute to change back into my regular clothes, and I'll be right down," I said.

"Aight then. I'll be back in a minute; I gotta run to the store right quick to get a blunt."

"To get a what?" I asked

"Never mind. Just go on down when you get done," she said before walking out and closing the bedroom door behind her.

I took off the attire and laid it across Chris's bed. I slipped my shapeless body back into my sweatsuit and walked downstairs. After thirty minutes, Darlene was done. I walked back upstairs, put on Chris's outfit, boots, some accessories, and make up. Now I was ready. I looked into the mirror, checking myself out.

"Damn, Nicole; you sexy," I said to myself before blowing an air kiss into the mirror. I walked away from the mirror feeling confident that tonight, I was going to enjoy myself.

Chapter Seventeen

"Just Trying To Have A Little Fun."

"Nicole? Reach inside of my purse and pull out the white envelope."

Taking a main street was the only way to get to the party quicker. Christyl clicked her signal light and drove into the right lane. As we quickly moved up the exit ramp, her demeanor became arrogant.

I reached inside her purse and pulled out the envelope.

"What's in here?" I looked inside the envelope and took the object from it. "Is this a blunt?"

"You know what the hell that is," she answered. "I made that one for us."

"What gave you the idea I smoked before? I never said anything about weed to you," I said to her.

"Well, I know you've been wanting to smoke some. You been telling me how your dad and his boys be smoking around you. Didn't the smell of it just make you want to try it?"

I didn't answer. I sat there staring out the passenger's window and thinking about Mike taking out his blunt before he died. Although I'd been around people who smoked a lot, the way weed felt in my system was never a thrill.

"My ex-boyfriend Mike was trying to get me to smoke some with him, but I never could," I said to her while examining the rolled-up drug.

"Mike? You ever mentioned Mike to me before?"

"Of course I have. This is the same Mike I used to get money from."

"Oh," she said, "how long were you two together?"

"We dated on and off for a couple of years. We were just starting to get along with each other before he got killed. Well, at least I thought we were," I said to her.

"Well, now you with me. We not gon' worry about that tonight. We gon' relax and have a good time with no worries, aight?" she said, passing me the lighter from her glove compartment. "When did you say he got killed?"

"In March," I repeated as I took the lighter from her hand to light one end of the blunt. I took a couple of hits and then passed it to her.

"No thanks, I'm already buzzing. I smoked some while you were getting your hair done."

"I was wondering what in the hell took you so long to go to the store." I said, laughing shamelessly. "Wait a minute…Please don't tell me you smoked a whole blunt by yourself?"

"Oh hell naw. I smoked it with my mother's boyfriend, Reggie." Chris said, taking a glance through her rear view mirror "That's who I buy it from."

After an odd moment of silence passed, she continued. "So tell me more about this Mike. How did he die?"

"It's a long story. All I can tell you is that two little boys found him in a parking lot dead, just lying in his truck, full of blood," I said while taking another hit. This time I took a longer and deeper hit. "That must have been some strong weed you was smoking, you losing your memory."

"Wait, wait—wait a minute! I think I do remember. Michael Nollings, right?"

"Yeah, that's his name," I answered.

After I gave it some thought, I stared at her casually, shook it off, and then hit the blunt again.

"Nick? I think I know him. Didn't he drive a black Escalade?" she asked.

"Yeah. As a matter of fact he did," I answered, holding the smoke in my throat.

"Oh my goodness, Nick, Was that your man?"

"Yep, that used to be my man."

Chris was sounding like she knew who he was. For all I knew, Chris could have been one of his girlfriends too—a girlfriend that I didn't know about. How did she know so much information about my Mike?

"Whoa, whoa, whoa. Hold up, Chris, wait a minute. How do you know so much about him?" I asked.

She stared through the windshield with a confused look upon her face before she continued.

"You must be high. Now *you're* the one that's losing her memory." she said

"Am I acting high?"

"Very." Chris said while making a left turn at the light. "And the thing about it is, they don't even know who did it. No witnesses around or nothing. They made it look like a suicide," she said, hitting her signal and making a turn.

"Yeah, but how do you know him, Chris?" I puffed the blunt one more time before putting the lit end out in the ashtray. I could feel the effect from the marijuana rising already. Rolling my window down for some fresh air was making me nervous.

Chris and I were silent for the next ten minutes. Even though the buzz became stronger and stronger, I was still waiting for her explanation and wondering how she knew Mike. I felt like I was waiting for hours.

Breaking the silence, I turned to her and asked, "Chris? Are you still high?"

"Hell yeah, that weed got some crystals in it," she informed me, rocking her head to the beat of "This is why I'm hot."

"You mean crystal meth?"

"Yup," she answered.

"I knew it felt different. Next time you buy some laced out weed, would you let me know before I inhale it? I should kick your rotten ass." I lifted my hand as if I was about to smack her, and she flinched.

"It's different from what? I thought you didn't smoke weed."

"Just different from what people say it's like," I answered.

"Girl, this weed ain't shit. I know it's a little stronger than what you're used to. But you will live."

At first I was mad at Chris for giving me some weed that had another drug mixed into it. But I was too stoned to get on her case. Plus, I felt good. My mouth became dry, sweat poured from my face, and the hot flashes and cramps in my stomach elevated. I was horny, nervous, and dizzy. But I was tight.

I closed my eyes and laid my head back. My mind begin to float into my childhood, then into my school, then straight to my friends, Mike, my fights with people, the incident with Harold, and my relationship with my mother in a matter of seconds. It was almost like looking at a glimpse of my life through a television screen with someone else holding the remote. After a few moments, I became nervous.

Chris's truck sped up. "I can beat this train. We're already late. I ain't got time to be waiting on no slow ass train."

"Chris? For real though, we should not be in this type of a hurry."

We were going 60 mph in a 25 mph zone. The train lights flashed as the gates were closing in. We had no choice but to slow down. It was either that or death.

Chris slammed her brakes to the metal; she was losing control of the steering wheel. After spinning around, we finally came to a complete stop. When we looked up, we were turned the same way the train was going.

"Sheee-it, I still say we could have made it."

After she turned the truck the right direction, she took the blunt out of the ashtray, grabbed a lighter, lit it, and took a hit. "This is some good shit. You want some more?"

"Don't you think you had enough, Chris? You out here high as hell in this geek town, racing trains. And you still got the nerve to be smoking some more. Gimme that!" I snatched the joint from her hand, placed it back into the envelope, and placed the envelope inside my pouch.

"I'm straight, Nick, why are you so bitchy tonight?"

"Do you think you can get us there without a scratch, Twinkie?"

She looked over at me and frowned. "Promise me you won't call me that when we get to the party."

"Call you what? Twinkie?"

"Yes, call me Twinkie. I hate that name, just like you hate Nicky."

"Okay, I promise," I concurred. "But promise me you won't do anything like that again. Next time you do this, and I live through it, you gon' be facing some serious hospital time. And I'm serious as hell."

She laughed, but I was for real. Too many incidents had occurred in my life that involved facing death, and I was tired of it.

When the train came to an end, Chris put the gear into drive and pulled off.

"Scaredy cat."

"Whatever, bitch."

Within minutes, we were parked in front of the house Kenny's party was at.

The music was bumpin'. Lots of people were moving their bodies to the beat and mingling around the front of the yard. Some of the guests were in their bathing suits; some were dressed normal.

"This seems like one of those freaky college parties," I said to Chris.

Chris overlooked my comment. She turned off the ignition, grabbed a small duffle bag from the back seat, and opened the car door. I got out of the car too and joined her at the front bumper of the truck. We strutted up the walkway in unison like two models on a runway. Chris was welcomed by friends and associates who stopped their own conversations just to talk to her. I started shaking. I was high on a drug and in a place where I knew not one living soul. All I asked was that Chris not leave me alone.

"Are you nervous?" she asked.

"No. do I look nervous?"

"A little," she said as she waved to a young girl who was sitting all by herself.

"I just hope I don't fall in these stilettos," I said, kicking my left foot back.

Chris held her right arm out and slid it underneath my left arm. "You'll be fine, Nicole. It looks to me like you know what you doing in those heels. You are actually working the hell out of those shoes." She laughed and gave me an elbow nudge at the same time. Then she released her arm.

We made our way to the back of the house. A tall, light-skinned, muscular man with a goatee slid toward Chris. He hugged and tongue kissed her with every force in his horny body.

"What's up baby? I missed you," he said after unlocking his lips from hers.

"I missed you too, baby." She threw her arms around his neck again. She pressed her lips against his for several more minutes before detaching herself. Finally, she wiped her mouth and introduced us to one other.

"Oh, baby, that is my girl, Nick. Nick, this is my man, Kenny."

"'Sup Nick. You aight?" He extended his hand for a handshake, and I accepted it.

"Oh yeah, I'm cool. And you?" I asked.

"Oh yeah, I'm cool too." His eyes studied my body from my head to my feet. When his eyes rolled up again to look me in the face, his head shook as if he was snapping himself back into reality.

"Aye, we got drinks, and we got the pool open just in case you wanna get that body wet." He pointed in the direction of the swimming pool. "And there's food in the kitchen. Why don't you help yourself to what you want, aight?" Kenny said to me.

"Thanks, Ken. I want to try those chicken wings I saw on this fella's plate. I started to snatch 'em off."

Kenny and I giggled in unison. But Chris didn't find that too amusing. She took her elbow and nudged Kenny in his side.

"I'll be back in a minute," I announced.

"Yeah, you go get your food," Chris announced, waving me off.

As I walked back through the yard, I felt good. The music was changing from a slow song to "Just Like Music" by Eric Sermon. Moving my body to the music and excusing myself through the crowd, I must have had confidence written on me. A cutie pie slid toward me and began moving his body in a motion corresponding with my body and the music.

"Come here, baby; I won't bite."

He, his body and his cologne enticed me. It was his breath that was throwing me off balance.

I moved my body seductively against his. He took a step forward, dancing closer to me. The nasty smell of his breath crossed my nose again. But instead of inhaling it, I did what any girl would do; I turned around and gave him some booty action.

Christyl and Kenny danced their way to the dance floor circle.

"Put it on him, Nick!" I heard Chris shout. The crowd moved in closer to watch.

With his arms clutching my waist, he pulled me closer to him. I felt his manhood rise and hit me on my thighs. I was curious, and with the hope of being clever, I bent my knees and dropped to the floor. On the way up, I was able to caress his dice with my hands.

Ooh-wee. I thought. *This man is blessed.*

"Now that's what I'm talking about," he said as he stumbled around trying to keep himself from falling over. The alcohol on his breath was making me nauseated. But oh! Was this man fine or what?

When the song ended, Chris and I slapped high fives and she returned to the yard where all Kenny's boys were standing. My handsome dance partner accompanied me to the garden area by hand. We sat down on the cement benches.

"So, cutie, What's your name?" he asked, taking a swig of his beer, "and where is your man at?" He looked around as if he was anticipating the arrival of another man.

"You think I would be dancing all on you like that if my man was around?"

"I just wanted to know. You ain't gotta get all sarcastic about it." He took another swig of his beer. "I'm Ice, by the way."

"Mine's Nick," I said, giving him a friendly smile. "How'd you get a name like Ice?"

"From all the ice I hold, baby," he responded, pointing to the silver and diamond links around his neck, the diamond watch on his wrist, the sterling silver diamond earring in his ear, and the baguette-filled bracelet on his other arm. I must admit that I was impressed with it from the time he pulled me to the side. But one of my laws of meeting a man is to not show him that I am impressed.

"So where is the weed?" he asked.

"What weed?" I asked.

"The weed you smoked. I smell it on you and you look high."

"I don't know what you're talking about," I said, denying his statement. I tried to turn the tables. "Are you drunk?"

"A little bit, but not really. Why?"

"Just asking."

He held his beer bottle up. "If you want one of these, I can go get it for you."

"I don't usually drink beer, but I'll try one. I'm not trying to get drunk from it, though."

"You already high off weed. I'm just imagining what yo' dancing would be like if you were drunk and high at the same time."

"That's why I don't need alcohol."

"Dang baby! Is it like that?"

"Can we stay focused here?" I asked, smacking my teeth.

"Oh, I'm focused. I'm definitely focused." He stopped to take another swig of his beer. "So, is there anything else I can get for you while I'm up, pretty lady?" He rose to his feet.

"Well I was on my way to get some of those chicken wings before you purposely held me hostage."

"Don't even try it. Ain't nobody holding you hostage. You jumped in front of me, remember?"

"Shit, did I?"

"Yes you did." He took another gulp of his beer. "I'm a go and get you a beer, aight?"

"That's cool." I really didn't want one, but since he was so anxious to get it for me, why not?

"Aight then. Be right back. Don't go anywhere."

He took another swig of his beer while strutting back into the house. I checked out his rear end and all the parts that a woman looks at. What I saw made me fantasize about doing some things.

Sliding next to me and giving me a shoulder bump, Chris broke my imagination. "Damn girl, look at you. You just got here and already you runnin' thangs."

"Oh pa-leeze, I'm just trying to have a little fun." I glanced over Chris's shoulder. "How's everything with you and Kenny?"

"He's over there talking to all his boys. Don't y'all wanna come over there with us?" she asked, pointing to the crowd where Kenny stood.

"Nope, I'll sit right here and have this man wait on me hand and foot. Shoot, I just might make him feed me. And when he's done, I'll let him rub my feet."

"Play on then, playa," she commented as we gave each other high fives again.

"So how long are we planning to be here?" I asked. "You know my dad would kill me if he knew I was out here."

"Not too long. I think I'll take Kenny away from his friends for a while. You know, to take care of some thangs. Will you be okay here for a moment by yourself?" she asked with sincerity.

"You see I got this under control. Go ahead and give your man a good time. I'll be fine here with Ice," I said to her.

"You sure? 'Cause I don't want you feeling uncomfortable."

"Will you go ahead and get your groove on. I'm chillin'. Just don't forget about me," I told her.

"How can I forget about you, Mami? You know you my dawg." She reached inside her push-up bra and took out her cellular phone. "Here, take this. Kenny's cell is programmed in here. Call me if you have to, aight? Just in case we take too long."

"Aight, but I should be tight for a while. You just go and have a good time."

"I don't see him that often. Especially now that he's moved out here. So when he gets home, or when I come down here, we just go for it."

"Oh yeah, no doubt about that. I understand."

"Fo' sho." She reached her arms out and gave me a quick hug. "Oh well, love you girl. See you in a minute."

"Love you too," I replied.

Chris looked up and saw Ice walking up from behind. She hopped to her feet and nodded toward his direction. "By the way, here comes your tall glass of Ice." She smacked her teeth and walked off smiling.

Ice walked up and sat down beside me. "Here you go, baby." He passed me the beer. "Who was that?"

"That's my dawg, Christyl," I answered.

"Is that her man over there? 'Cause one of my boys wanted to holla at her," he said, still focusing faintly in Chris's direction.

"Tell yo' boy she got a man. And she's about to go break him off some," I told him as I tried to unscrew the top off of my beer bottle. I had no luck, so I held it in my hand.

"Damn. So my boy don't stand a chance with that dime piece, huh?" he asked, taking a swig at his beer.

"I doubt it." I picked up his hands. "Boy, where's my chicken wings?"

"Dammit! I knew I forgot something. You know what? I'm going back into the house to get you some chicken wings, aight?"

"You know what, Ice? Don't worry about it. It just wasn't meant for me to have those wings." I gestured.

"Well why don't I make it up to you? Why don't I just take you out to dinner one day and you can get all the chicken you want?"

I leaned back, giving him an investigative look. "I might have to take you up on that offer."

"So, what do you want to do now?" he asked

"Why don't we do a little ballroom dancing. Some stimulating conversations would be respectable. And don't tell me you don't know how to ballroom dance?"

I reached over to grab the half-empty beer bottle from his hand and set it to the side. I tugged at him as a indication that I wanted him to dance with me again.

The R. Kelly song "Step in the name of love" was now playing, and people were dancing again.

"Yeah, I know what to do. The question is Do *you* know how to ballroom?" he initiatorily asked.

"I know that I know what I'm doing. Just don't drag me out there and you don't know what you're doing. If you can't ballroom, we might as well sit here and drink beer all afternoon instead of going over there and embarrassing ourselves."

"Girl, come on out here and let me see what you got." He grabbed my hand and led me toward the dance floor circle.

Chapter Eighteen

"The Wrong Dance."

With his warm hands planted on my hips, he stepped next to me, making sure our rhythm was good before throwing me outward. He pulled me in. We waltzed our way into the cha-cha step, then the temptation walk, then the side-to-side step, and we paused. We sashayed, doing hand-over-hand moves, women-in-the-cradle moves, and hesitation moves, demonstrating the simplicity of the ballroom hustle.

When he finally took my body in for a dip, my whole body yearned for his touch. We made a good team. At that moment, I felt a spark between us. Then a question was uprooted:

"Lord, did I find my soul mate?"
And I waited patiently for the answer.

It was getting late and the crowd was dying down. Chris and Kenny hadn't come back from their love encounters yet. I decided to hang around with Ice until then.

I opened Christyl's flip phone, searching through the phone book area for Kenny's number. Instead of Kenny's name, I came across the name "future hubby." I remembered her calling Kenny "my future hubby" when I was trying on clothes at her house. I pressed the call button, and the lines connected:

"Hello," The sleepy and deep voice spoke from the other end of the phone.

"Um, hey, this is Nick. I was just calling to check on Chris. Is she still there?"

"Who in the hell is Nick?" he asked.

"This is Nicole. I know that it's a lot of music in the background, but you can still hear me, right?

"Yeah I hear you. I want to know who in the hell this is calling my house this late asking for Chris. Don't no Chris live here," he said.

"Wait a minute; whose number did I call?" I asked in confusion. This didn't sound like Kenny; this kind of sounded like Darlene's boyfriend. Later on, I learned that Reggie was some man that she had been messing around with on the down low, but she hadn't talked to him recently because he had a new girlfriend

"This is Reggie. And no, Chris is not here. Don't call my house again," he said, and then he hung up.

I shook it off.

Without a second thought about that call, I searched through the phone book of Chris's phone again. This time I looked for Kenny's name, knowing that this was what I should have done in the first place. Finally, I found it. I pushed the call button. It started to ring. Only this time there was no answer.

I pressed the redial button two more times. It rang, but there was still no answer. I waited until the greeting on the voicemail to end before leaving a message.

"Hi Chris—or Kenny. This is Nick. I'm still here at the party waiting on you two to finish doing whatever it is you do. Please pick up the freakin' phone if you will. Or call me on this phone and let me know something. Bye!"

As Ice slid back to the table, I was just hanging up.

"Hey Nick, I'm 'bout to go back to my apartment. Have you heard anything from yo' girl yet?" he asked.

"I'm trying to reach her now, but her ass won't pick up the phone," I told him. I dialed Kenny's cellular number for the fourth time, and still there was no answer.

"You know what, shorty? I still owe you dem chicken wings, right?"

"Yeah you do," I said bluntly. "I'm sitting here starving to death, and it's all your fault. I should have gotten some wings when I had the chance."

"Well, why don't we go get some now. We'll be back in time, or at least before Chris comes back. Or we can get a room and just chill until yo' girl is ready. I'll bring you back here. I promise," he said while sliding his hands on my back and rubbing my neck.

I was getting frustrated, and at the same time, I wanted to chill with him. I knew he wanted some booty, and I can admit that I was a little horny too. But I knew that if we went to his place right now, we would probably end up doing something.

"I guess it would be aight," I told him. "You promise you'll bring me back here?"

"I promise. Do I look like the type that would try to kidnap you?"

I know one thing is for sure: you don't have to look like a kidnapper to be one. Even if he didn't look harmless.

Determined to find Chris, I called Kenny's cell phone one more time. It was the fifth time I had tried. I left another message telling her where I was going. After that, I snapped the flip phone shut, tossed it into my purse, and decided to have a good time for myself until they were ready to go.

We got inside of his car. He drove a dark-colored Cutlass Supreme with dark-colored tinted windows. On the bottom of his doors, he had silver mirrors made of glass with silver trimmings. His engine's hood had a picture of the number one made of ice. This car was decent, but with the way he was dressed, I thought that we would be getting into a Lexus, or at least a Benz.

Ice-One took me to a place where he claimed the chicken wings are off the hook. After ordering a dozen of them with chili fries and a salad, we decided to go to a nearby hotel about four blocks from the party. He says that his room mate snores to loud. We wouldn't be able to have any privacy.

When we got to our room, I turned the television on and ordered my favorite movie "Training Day" with Denzel's fine ass. I sat down at the table and pulled the rest of the joint Chris gave me from my purse.

"You wanna hit this?" I asked as I lit it, hit it and passed it to him.

"Oh naw baby, I'm tight. I'm a drinker, not a smoker. You wouldn't believe what people put in the weed these days."

"You wouldn't believe what people put in drinks these days." I told him hunching my shoulders "Its only Crystal Meth mixed in with it. Try it"

"Nuh-uh baby, I'm going to hook me up a drink. You want me to hook you up one too?" he asks, as he got up and walked over to the dining table. "And if you don't mind, you can give me a little lap dance if you feel like it."

"A lap dance huh?" I smacked my teeth and said "I think my feet are done dancing for tonight."

"Yeah, okay. We shall see baby, we shall see," he said to himself.

I took a couple more puffs of the joint and placed the rest of it in my purse. I sat at the table to eat my chicken wings while licking my fingers. I was feeling the effects from the joint until all my food was gone. Ice-One broke my flow with his impression of Ceilie and Nettie's father from *The Color Purple*.

"Ain't you done yet?" he asked.

"Yes Ice, I'm ready to watch the movie now." I got up, threw the box in the trash, and sat down on the bed next to him.

"Sho' took you long enough." He snapped. "I fixed you a drink." He leaned over, grabbed the drink from the nightstand, and passed it to me. "Here, try it."

"This drink is tight. What's in it?" I asked, licking my lips.

"Malibu and pineapple juice. You like it?

"Yeah, it has a good taste to it. I never tried Malibu before," I said. I took another sip.

"Glad you like it."

I snuggled under his arm. Ice began rubbing the back of my neck and messaging my shoulders. He moved his hand toward my breast. I smacked his hand and placed it back on my neck.

"We don't have to do anything if you don't want to. I can respect that," he said to me.

I leaned over and gave him a kiss on the cheek. "It's just not the right time right now." I picked up my Malibu and finished it off.

It wasn't long before I was feeling dizzy, nauseated and light headed. The room became hot and was dramatically spinning out of control.

"Damn baby, I don't feel so good," I told him as I tried to sit up, but I couldn't move.

"You just can't handle your liquor, that's all. It's just Malibu." He laid the back of his hand on my forehead "You gon' be aight." He patted me on the back and turned his attention to the television.

"No. Wait a minute…something's not right."

"You need to stop," Ice-One said, chuckling.

"I'm for real. My head is spinning, and I feel hot."

"Well, stretch out on the bed and lay your head back."

"Yeah, I think I should do that. Let me call Chr—" I tried to stand up and walk to the dining table to get the cell phone, but I lost my balance. Ice jumped to his feet. He threw my arms around his neck, helped me back to the bed, took off my shoes, and covered me with a blanket.

"I'll bring you some ice water and a cold towel. I'll be right back, aight? You just lay there and chill."

"Mmhm," I mumbled.

The sweat poured down my face, and I could no longer feel my legs. The room began to spin. Within minutes I was in a deep sleep. I could still hear what was going on in the room, but I swear it was like I was in a coma.

I never got that cup of water he offered. In fact, when I woke up, I looked around the room for him and the water, and Ice was nowhere to be found. I was naked with blood flowing from my legs and the bed sheets. Not remembering for the life of me what happened while I was asleep, I lay on the bed trying to shake it off. My mouth was sticky and dry, and my body reeked of a bad odor. After struggling to sit up, it dawned on me—I had been drugged and raped.

I picked up the phone and called the front desk. I told the clerk that I had been raped, laid the phone down on the bed, and waited for someone to rescue me from this tragic moment.

Chapter Nineteen

"WE MET IN GOOD TIMING"

I managed to finish school with flying colors, but only because Chris brought home my assignments. It felt good to march across the stage, kissing these high-school years goodbye. Now that this part was over, it was time to start getting my future together. My plan for my life was to not end up like my mother said I would, but to do better. I owed it to myself to prove her wrong.

Ice-One could not be traced. He had pretended like he attended Bowling Green College and used a fake ID to rent the room. No one knew who he was, not even Kenny. But they remembered what he looked like. Kenny told me that if he ever saw Ice-One, he would beat him down for me. That's funny. That is the same thing my father told me about Harold. None of this would have happened if I'd stayed my ass at home.

I went to the hospital that morning and was released that next evening, and decided to stay with Chris. It was a good thing Darlene and Reggie went to Hawaii that next day. That was really in the nick of time.

I told Papa G I was going to stay with Chris for a few days. That way I will have more time to recover. After all was said and done, I ended up moving in with Chris. I never told Papa G what happened.

"Can you believe we are officially done with high school?" Chris asked, taking off her graduation cap and gown and throwing them on her bed.

"I told you we were going to make it, Chris," I said, taking my cap and gown and tossing them on the bed next to hers. I sat down at the pink-colored vanity mirror next to her pink couch. My back was turned toward Chris, but I could see her reflection through the vanity mirror. "I don't know why you worried."

"I was scared, Nicole."

"Scared of what?"

"I was afraid you weren't going to make it."

"I know," I condoled. "I thank God for you, Chrystal. I couldn't have made it without you. You really were there for me."

"You know I couldn't have made it without you too, Nick," she said

Chris plopped down on her pink sofa. She ripped her high-heeled pumps from her feet and gave her feet a personal message. "Why didn't your mother show up? What is her problem?"

"I don't know why she didn't come. I sent her an invitation, and I didn't receive a card or a call from her," I said, shaking my head in shame.

"Well, at least Papa G still loves you enough to show up," she told me. "Sorry it didn't work out while you were living with him."

"I'm straight. I love Pop, but I can't live with him. He was too dirty."

"But it's good my brother moved out. That's when we had the extra room for you."

Chris slipped into her nightgown, straightened out her goose-feather blanket, and dived on the bed to lie down.

I sat at her vanity mirror in silence, staring at the reflection of a high-school graduate. This is amazing. Out of all the things that happened to me, through the grace of God, I still made it through.

"I still don't get it, Chris," I said as I leaned back in the chair.

"Get what?" she mumbled with her eyes closed.

"We are good friends, aren't we?"

"Yeah, of course. I wouldn't let just anyone move in with me."

"See, that's my point. How did we become close friends? It feels like all I ever did was borrow." I said.

"You tripping, Nick. Go to sleep," she said, shifting her head from one side to the other on her pillow.

"No, I'm serious, Chris. You ever stop to think how a person like me and you just all of a sudden got a connection with each other?"

She shifted her head on the pillow to face in my direction and opened her eyes. "Well, I'll put it to you like this: There are lots of friends that come and go. Most of them try to impress me because they know I have money. They act stuck-up just to prove something to me. I don't think of myself the way most people think I should think about myself. I'm blessed to have what I have. I don't let it go to my head. I don't try to impress people. I don't try to be something I'm not." She sat up in her bed and continued. "Then there are those I run into who are jealous of me because I have money. These are the ones that act like monks toward me."

"I don't know why. You are such a beautiful person with confidence in herself," I told her.

She pointed her fingers at me and winked. "See, that is why I love you." She lay back down and tossed the comforter over her head.

After a brief moment, I broke the silence. "I still want to know how we became so close."

She sat up in her bed again. This time, she removed the covers completely, put her feet to the floor, walked over to the couch next to me, and sat down. She leaned over, looked me straight in the eyes, and said, "I knew from the moment you tried to help me in Ms. Whittlemoore's class that you were cool and that you had a sense of humor. You are who you are, and that was good enough for me. You were being yourself and you weren't trying to impress me. On that day, I saw your heart, and I still see it"

"Yeah, I'm me. I can't be no one else. It takes up too much time and energy to be fake," I said.

"And that's what I love about you, Nick. From that point on, I felt connected with you. God knows I was tired of the fake friends. I just got tired of all that, and I knew I needed someone real in my life—someone I could talk to, share everything, and just be friends with other than fashion advice. People with money get lonely too. Plus, God knew I needed help with my French, and you were the master in it," She said, flashing me a smile.

"I love French, too. I just flunked out because of the circumstances around me."

"That's my whole point. God put us together when we needed each other," she said, sitting back in her chair. "I needed you and you needed me. That's how we became friends. God's timing is perfect."

"Yeah, but can you explain what happened to me? I mean—I'm just saying—I keep having these thoughts that if I hadn't 've met you, I never would have gone to that party, and I never would have gotten raped."

Chris sat back in the couch, wondering just how something so reckless could happen. A frown arose on her face and she threw her hands up. "I haven't the slightest clue. All I know is that you and I are here now. We have become closer to one another. I just wish Kenny would find this Ice-One person. Then it would have solved a lot of grief. I know people who could walk straight up in his crib and get his ass put out of his own misery."

"Oh yeah! Me too. I hope one day somebody catch ahold of him and give him what's coming to him, " I said, grabbing one of Chris's make up cleansing pads from the desktop and wiping the make up smudges from my face.

"Sooner or later, he'll get his. As soon as you forgive someone, they'll start paying for what they've done to you. Sometimes you get to see them pay, and sometimes you don't."

"Well, I would love to see him cry like a lil' bee-otch when a 450-pound gorilla busts his ass open when he go to jail, 'cause you know that's where he's headed."

"Hun! Be careful what you ask for; you just might get it," she said. "You might not want to be in jail watching that." She stood up from the couch, dove back into her bed, and pulled the huge comforter over her. "It's hot as hell in here, too. Do you mind opening a window or something?"

"Uh-uh Chris. If you take that hot ass feathered blanket off your bed and switch it for something thinner, you might be able to breathe a little better," I said to her. I grabbed the pink Hello Kitty pillow from the couch and bopped her with it. I wasn't ready for her to fall asleep. I wanted to talk some more.

"Ouch!"

She jumped out of the bed, laughing. She grabbed another pillow and threw it in my direction, but it missed.

Chapter Twenty

"In God we trust."

Summer ended and fall began. We were so desperate to find something to do with ourselves that we decided to do some job hunting. There were companies that wanted to hire us to either wash their dishes or mop their floors, but Chris's expectation was higher. She refused to take anything that consisted of grease, cleaning up someone else's mess, or outside door-to-door sales. I don't mind taking a job like that right now, but not having transportation left me with no choice.

We found a job working at the Hyatt Regency Hotel. It paid every week, but the first check came after two weeks. This left us a check in the hole. One of Darlene's clients used to work midnights there, and she informed us of the front desk positions. We didn't have to take a drug test or a stupid assessment test to get in. All we needed was a driver's license and a social security card. They didn't care whether we had past experience or not.

The hotel had rooms that cost anywhere between $150 and $300 per night. They were equipped with top-of-the-line bed coverings, paintings, and carpeting. Some of the suites even had kitchen areas. Even better, when Chris and I decided to take our two-week vacation, we would get free accommodations.

Chris and I got our first checks. We drove home to her house. She pulled her cherry-red Cherokee truck into the driveway and turned the key backwards so that we could listen to "When You're Mad" by that fine singer Ne-Yo.

"My first paycheck," Chris announced while taking it out of the envelope and kissing it. "Feels good to make my own money."

"Let me see how much yours is." I snatched the check out of her hand. "My check is $12 more than yours. How did that happen?"

"I don't know, but I can give you six dollars from it so we can be even," she answered.

"Yeah, give me six dollars," I said, holding my hand out.

"I'm not giving you nada," she said.

"But I thought you said—"

"Sorry, I don't give away money."

As we sat in the Jeep looking at our checks, my thoughts drifted to what Ice-One did to me at the hotel. It made me nauseated. "I wish somebody could tell me that Ice-One is dead."

"Aw damn!" she grunted.

"Aw damn what?" I asked.

"Here you go again worrying about him. That punk is going to get his. Don't worry about it."

"I know Chris, it's just hard." Tears began forming in my eyes.

Chris threw her arms around my shoulders and kissed me on the cheek. "Let us get outta the car, change out of these work uniforms, go to the bank, and do some shopping. You need a makeover; maybe that would make you feel better." She took the keys from the ignition and grabbed her purse. "Let's get outta here and spend some money. Now you can finally get a cell phone."

"Whatever."

At the mall, we stopped by the food court first. I ordered my usual: chicken wings, fries, and lemonade. Chris ordered a chicken salad special with ranch dressing and a raspberry iced tea. After lunch, we looked around at several stores. I bought two pairs of denim jeans from The Gap, a pair of dress slacks, a pair of Banana Republic boots, some lingerie from Victoria's Secret, and would you believe…a cell phone?"

We walked inside a department store that had everything from clothes and shoes on the upper level to lawnmowers and barbecue grills on the lower level. We walked over to the make up station to get ourselves facial makeovers. Then we walked over to the jewelry section to look at their diamond selections. I looked inside one of the showcases. In there was the ring of my dreams. It was a ½ carat diamond wedding band.

"Which one you like?" the Asian sales associate behind the counter asked in her cultural accent.

"This one right here," I said, pointing to the one I desired.

She took the ring from the showcase and placed it into my hand. I tried it on my left-hand ring finger. It was a perfect fit.

"How much is this ring, ma'am?" I asked her.

"These one a cost a-youabout two tousin dolla. You want buy?"

"I love it, but no thanks. I'm just looking for now." I took the ring off and placed it back into her hands.

"Maybe you tell fiancé come down and get for you; I give him good deal. Yeah?" she said, answering her own question.

"Okay, I'll do just that, thank you," I told her. Chris was staring at the silver bracelets on the other end of the showcase.

"Nick? Come and look at these little diamond friendship bracelets. They remind me of things we did in elementary school." She looked around for the Asian sales clerk, "Uh, excuse me miss, can I see these two bracelets right here? I want to know how much they are," Chris said, tapping on the glass to point it out.

"I get for you. I give you good deal. Which one you like?" The Korean saleswoman looked through the showcase to see which bracelets Chris was pointing to. She opened the window, carefully taking the bracelets from the tray. She flipped the price tag over and then handed the jewelry to Chris. "20 percent off both out the door if you pay cash now. No lay-way. You want buy, yeah.?"

"20 percent huh? Well do I have to pay with cash? I mean, can I use a credit card instead?"

"I take credit card, yeah," she answered.

"Okay, yeah, I'll take them both. No need to wrap it; we'll just wear ours out of the door," Chris told her. Chris picked up one of the bracelets off the showcase counter and began snapping the bracelet around my wrist.

"See if this fits your arm first of all."

"It's a little tight, but I think it's cool." I told her.

"They're both the same size, so If yours fits your arm, then I know that mine will fit." She took her credit card out of her purse and passed it to the Asian sales clerk. The cashier swiped it and passed it back to Chris.

"Tank you, have nice day."

"Thank you, and you do the same," We both said in unison, and then we walked toward the exit door.

Chris opened the exit door, letting me out first. I looked up and saw my mother entering the store with her stomach huge and her purse swinging at her side.

"Mommy dearest?" I asked in shock. The sight of her at the mall by herself surprised me.

"Hi Nicole, How are you?" she sternly asked without breaking her stride. I reached out my arms and gave her a warm hug. She barely hugged me back.

"You look nice. When's the baby due?" I asked.

"In two months," she replied.

"Two months. Dang, has it been that long already? Seems like you just told me you were pregnant."

"I guess so," she answered. She hunched her shoulders before looking over them. "Have you seen Harold around?"

"No, I haven't seen him." My money was on my mind. I wanted to ask her about it, but somehow it didn't seem like the right time.

"Who is this?" Isis asked, pointing at Chris.

"Oh, this is my friend Chris. Chris, this is Isis—my mother." Chris extended her hand for a handshake.

"Nice to meet you, Ms. Isis."

"Um, yeah, likewise." she replied. Isis looked at Chris's hand and then lifted her hand to accept it.

I could tell Chris felt uneasy. Her eyebrows lifted from her eyes and she took a deep breath. "Um, Okay...uh...Nick, I'll leave you two alone. I'll be at that shoe store over there when you're ready."

"Okay." I winked my eye. I understood her awkward feeling.

"So is that you're new lover, or is it just somebody you're trying to get jewelry from?" Isis asked.

"What? Chris is a friend I met in school, and why are you even asking me that?"

I thought I knew where she was taking me. It was one of those roads where everything seemed to go so well at first and you think you are on your way to your destination. But out of the blue, you realize that there is a brick wall in the road and your brakes just went out on you.

"I'm talking about you. I see those little bracelets y'all have on. I know she bought them 'cause I know how broke you are. When are you going to stop itching off people?"

I took a deep breath through my nostrils and released it. I knew it was coming, so I said nothing. I shut my mouth and let her continue.

"And how can you leave your mother like this? You just took off one day and didn't come back. You don't call anymore. You don't care about anyone but yourself. You treat me like dirt—your own mother. How can y—?"

"Oh pa-lease, stop the drama!" I said, cutting into her full-mouthed criticism. " I can't take no more. You know what, Mom? For your information, I graduated, okay? I got a new job, and I'm about to get my own place. I bought these clothes for myself as well as these boots. I haven't called you and asked you for anything since I've been gone. All the brutal words you spoke, all the pain and grief you put me through. You know what? I love you, and you're all I have, but with all due respect, I refuse to stand here and listen to you talk to me about how sorry I am, when you're the one sitting at home with a boyfriend who rapes your daughter and you did nothing about it."

She shifted her weight onto her other side. Her eyes bulged and her lips turned up. "You don't talk to m—"

"I'm not done," I said. "And you're the one who lets this man do anything he wants to do in your own house. You let Mike use me and you let Harold take advantage of me. And where is the money I put in my mattress? Huh? Somebody had to see it."

"See how you disrespect me like this out in public? You use this kind of language and you think you ju—"

"G'bye, Momma," I said to her, lifting my palms into her face. "I gotta go. I see you haven't changed one bit. You know what? Keep that money. The way I look at it, It's a nice gift to my little sister or brother." I turned around and walked in the direction where Chris was now standing. Isis called me by my middle name.

"Salina, wait!" She walked toward me. She only called me Salina when she needed me to do something or when she was trying to call a truce. "Look, Harold is in and out of jail a lot. So he hasn't been able to make much money. My food stamps stopped, so I haven't been able to eat right. Plus, I received a letter in the mail telling me that they were going to stop my social security checks soon. Family services won't even give me a cash grant 'cause I owe them money. I can't fit into any of my clothes. No one will hire a pregnant woman. I don't know what to do." Her eyes got strange, and her face had no expression. I took a closer look at her as she was talking, and I noticed a scar right behind her left ear. It was obvious that Harold put it there. His name was written all over it.

"What part of that is my problem? You made your bed and now you have to lie in it."

"But Salina, I know what I did to you was wrong, and I'm sorry. But I'm still your mother."

For a brief moment, I was speechless. I took a second look in the direction Chris went just to see if she was standing there watching me. I opened my purse, took out my wallet, and asked with a sigh, "So how much do you need?"

"I need at least two hundred dollars."

Two hundred dollars? She didn't want to hug me when she saw me and she blew Chris off like she was dust on a coffee table. She wants me to give her something I worked hard for. On top of all that, who was to say when I'd get it back? This meant I would have to give her the rest of the money from my paycheck. Should I put my name in the "Guinness Book of World Records" for the world's stupidest daughter? What I was tripping off of was that she still hadn't said anything about the money in my mattress. That is what was making me furious.

"Here, take it." I shoved it into her hands "I wish the best for you."

I walked away feeling sorry for her. She could have told me she loved me. She could have given me congratulations on my graduation. At least that would have made me feel halfway loved.

All I could do was do what my heart told me to do.

Isn't it funny how people treat their own flesh and blood and end up needing them in the end?

Chapter Twenty-one

"Foul tongue, smooth move."

Two years later...

Chrystal and I are still working at the hotel. We've gotten three raises in our salary, a new apartment, and we are leasing brand new cars.

Our two-bedroom, two-bathroom apartment is a nice start for us. It may not be much to anybody else, but to us, our apartment was laced. Everything we needed to survive was right there in the apartment (except for our jobs, of course). It had a carport garage, a washing machine and dryer, a dishwasher, a garbage disposal, a refrigerator, and an electric stove. And just in case we wanted to work out, there was a fitness center downstairs, a sauna, a hot tub, and a nice-sized pool. For our own first apartment, we were living fabulously and fashionably.

Chris and I had the Christmas holiday weekend off. We decided to do the cooking at our house. Yesterday we pre-cooked the greens, spaghetti, salad, and green beans. This morning we made the macaroni and cheese, the ham, and the turkey. The only thing missing were the decorations.

We got into the car and drove to the nearest WalMart store. WalMart was the spot for us. This place was off the hook, especially on holidays.

Chris was getting frustrated. She thought that the extra registers are open and you are in and out in a jiffy around this time of year.

"Come on, this is ridiculous." Chris pouted.

"I thought you picked this stuff up last month. I should've known that you were going to wait until the last minute,"

"I've noticed something about you, Nicole. You like to learn things the hard way."

"Oh, shut the hell up." I said "Fuck this, we need to leave all of these decorations right here in this store and forget about this."

"Excuse me?" A soft yet manly voice from behind asked. "Those lips of yours are far to beautiful to let those kind of words flow from it."

I felt a strong energy rush through my entire body. There was something about his energy that gave me the adrenaline rush. Nothing could compare to this.

The first things I noticed were his chocolate-coated lips. They reminded me of a honey-coated Hershey's chocolate caramel kiss wrapped in silk. His mocha-colored skin was without a scratch, and his hazel eyes stared at me from head to toe.

"Hoo-we," I said, staring at him from head to toe as well.

Chris elbowed me in the side. "Talk to him," she mumbled.

He cleared his throat. "Your lips are to beautiful for those kind of words," he repeated. I felt myself standing in front of him with a stupid look on my face. I was too deep into his eyes to figure out what the hell he just said. I enjoyed watching his lips move. Chris felt uncomfortable with the silence between us. She jumped in and made the craziest comment.

"You would be surprised at what else could come out of this girl's mouth," she remarked.

I took my eyes off of him and gave Chris a strong look, as if she was eating dog food with chopsticks. Then she continued.

"I mean...well...She can speak French and hold intelligent conversations when she's not mesmerized over a georgeous man—things like that," she added.

"Is that so?" he asked, staring down at me. His eyes never left mine. I stood there under his tall physique like a toddler looking up at her father.

"I speak a little French," I said in support of her compliment.

"I speak French too," he added.

"Oh really?"

"Yes really."

"Well, say something in French," I requested. We stood still for several seconds in silence. Our eyes were still focused on one another.

"Tell me what you want to hear, and I will be more than happy to translate it for you."

"Just say anything. Tell me how your day was."

"*C'etait bon, Merci beaucoup.*" As the words gracefully flowed out of his heart-shaped lips, my legs shivered.

"What did you just say about your bones?" Chris interrupted. She was now looking through a magazine with Tyrese's picture on the front cover.

"He just told me that he is having a good day. Then he thanked me very much." I explained to Chris without taking my eyes off of him.

Chris asked, "How do you say 'open up another cash register up in this piece so we can bounce up out this be-ach?'"

"*Pourez vous ouvir l'outre caisse, S'il vous plait. A fin de pouvoir sortir d'ici.*" His French was sharp and his accent sounded smooth. This man is not only the sexiest man in this store, but the way this language rolled off of his tongue made me want to kiss him, just to see what his words tasted like.

"*Je ne parler pas en francais, et, je ne comprende pas le francais beaucoup,*" Chris said

"What is your girl trying to say?" he asked.

"She said that she doesn't speak French, and she doesn't understand a lot of it either," I whispered.

"Oh." He hunched his shoulders before he asked me another question in French. "*Comment tu appelles, mon cherie?*"

"My name is Nicole, but my friends call me Nick," I answered in English.

"You mean, like Nicky-Nick?"

"It's not Nicky," I told him bluntly. The word *Nicky* broke the ice. After I stepped back away from him, I realized I had been in his face for three and a half minutes, which is a long time for me to be up in somebody's face when I don't know who they are.

"Whatever you do, don't call me Nicky. Please! Don't call me Nicky. I hate that damn name."

"Okay, I won't," he said politely. "But you would have to promise me that you won't do that again." He said in a most sincere tone.

"Do what again?" I asked, unless he was reading the dirty thoughts I had of him being naked, I wondered what the hell I could have done to offend him.

"You cursed again."

"I did what?" I asked.

Chris turned around. "Yeah girl, you said 'damn.' It's obvious—this man is allergic to curse words. I saw that from the moment you used the first one," she said, and then she continued pulling coupons out of her purse.

I scoffed.

"Well, I'm Darren. Unfortunately, I don't have a *nick*name like you do."

"Well, what do you have?" I asked.

"A lot of things."

"Things like what?"

"Like joy, peace, and serenity."

"Uh huh," I replied.

I wasn't sure I wanted his number at that point.

I reached into my purse and pulled out the money for my half of the grocery bill and passed it to Chris. She gave the money to the cashier, took the receipt, and tucked it inside her purse.

"Okay Nicole, We are all set to go," Chris said. "It was nice talking to you in French, Darren. I hope to see you again one day."

He looked at me and said, "I'm sure we will."

Chris put the bags into the car while I sulked in the driver's seat.

"Why didn't you get his number, stupid?" Chris said as she got into the car.

"Don't know. He didn't ask me for mine, so I didn't ask him for his," I said.

Chris shook her head. "You so smooth."

Chapter Twenty-two

"Unwholesome Giving."

"What time did your father say he was coming over?" Chris asked. "Does he know what time he is supposed to be here?"

"Who knows," I answered, opening a stick of gum and placing it in my mouth.

"Shouldn't you call him?"

"I guess," I told her.

Chris pulled my cell phone from my purse and dialed his number before passing it to me.

"Here's your daddy, ask him."

I rolled my eyes and chuckled before snatching the phone from her hand.

"Hey, baby girl. How is everything?"

"Good," I told him. During the brief pause, the pounding noise in the background became noisier. "And how are you doing?"

"I'm doing pretty good over here for an old man," he answered. The hammering and knocking was so loud that Chris could hear it from her passenger seat.

"That is a lot of racket in the background, Pop, what are you doing?" I asked.

"We are trying to patch up a roof."

"Patch up a roof? On a holiday?" I asked.

"Yeah, baby, on a holiday. Ms. Payton from next door called this morning and said she was about to start cooking when her kitchen ceiling started to leak. I couldn't tell her no."

I looked at my watch. "But will we still see you around four thirty?"

"four thirty it is. We are over here starving too," he added.

"We got plenty to eat here."

"What did you cook?"

"Just what is it that you are expecting?"

"Anything but beans and rice will do us fine." We both let out snickers.

"Don't worry. You are about to eat good for a change. Chris and I downloaded some recipes from the internet. And plus, I've been watching Isis cook."

"I trust you." He let out a big yawn before he continued. "Speaking of Isis, have you talked to her lately?"

"I haven't talked to her since I saw her at the mall two years ago. I would like to know if I have a little sister or a little brother," I said, hitting my signal lights and waiting for traffic to clear so I could make my left turn.

"You do what you're heart tells you to do, Nicole. Does she have your cell or your house number?"

"No. But she does have Darlene's number. I'm sure if she called, Darlene would have given her my cellular number. I know Darlene would tell me if Isis called,"

"What is up with your mama? I didn't think she would still be acting like this," he said.

"I'm okay with her just staying out of my life. She wasn't doing jack for me anyway."

"Nicole, look now. You gone have to watch your language," he demanded. "She is still your mother you know?"

I stopped when I heard Tony's voice shouting from the background.

Pops covered the mouthpiece as he hollered to his friend. "I'm coming down to take care of that Tony, just leave it alone, man." He put his mouth back up to the phone. "Okay, baby girl. I got a situation over here. I'll see you guys soon. And tell Chris I said hello."

I looked over at the passenger seat where Chris sat. She was scanning the cash register receipt and frowning.

"Pop said 'Hi,' Chris," I said to her.

"Hey Pop!" she shouted loud enough that he could hear her, without taking her eyes off of the receipt paper.

"Aight Pops, We are on our way home. I don't like to talk and drive at the same time. I'll see you guys in a minute."

"Okay hon. Love you."

"Love you too, Pops."

"Nick, will you look at this receipt? The cashier was so frustrated she just stuck some of the stuff into our bags and didn't charge us for it. Looks like we saved ourselves about twenty bucks."

"Okay nah why you let that girl do that? That's called stealing, you know."

"No the hell it ain't," she bluntly announced. "If she stuck those items into our bags and didn't charge us for 'em, that's not stealing; that's called getting shit for free. Ya heard?"

"Whatever you say," I said to her. "I know that *I* didn't steal it, so what is the point of me even arguing?"

"Me neither," she added. "Even though its stolen merchandise."

"So don't I get $10 back out of that?" I asked, holding out my right hand toward her.

Chris reached in her purse and took out a ten-dollar bill. "You sure do."

I grabbed the money and stuck it into my pocket. "Thank you, ma'am."

"Ooh, Nick, we forgot to pick up the hamburger for the spaghetti," she said, "and we forgot the salad dressing for the salad. We need napkins and some paper plates too. Damn! We might as well turn around and head back to the grocery store."

"We can't."

"Why?"

"Not enough time, and don't forget we have food in the stove warming up as we speak."

"Drop me off and I'll be watching the food while you go get the rest of the stuff. That way I can be putting up the décor, boiling the noodles, and all. If we both go together, there's no telling how long we'd be standing in line at the grocery store, so—"

"That's fine with me. I can help you take the stuff up. I got to come in anyway to use the bathroom."

"Cool," she said. "So you say your dad's two friends are coming along too, huh?"

"Yeah, they'll be there."

"They must not be married, because if they were, wouldn't their wives be cooking for them?"

"I guess so," I answered. There was a brief pause, and Chris was looking like she was thinking hard about something.

"How do Tyrone and Anthony look? Are they cute?"

"You talking about them old-ass men dad roll with? I dunno what cute look like at that age," I told her.

I pulled into the complex and into our carport. We grabbed the bags, locked the car doors with the remote on my keys, and went inside. I looked in the refrigerator, hoping to find some hamburger that we may have overlooked, but there was no luck. I grabbed my keys, the credit card, and my license and drove over to the nearby grocery store. I walked inside and went to the meat department for the hamburger. I picked up some onions and peppers to put in the spaghetti. Then I headed over to the cash register where there was only one person in line. I was next to being served. *This is a lot better than that other store we went to. I can be in and out of here in no time.* I thought.

An older man at the front of the line was patting his pants pocket and looking for his wallet. It was not there.

"My wallet is in the car," The gray-haired senior citizen announced. "My car is parked right there." He pointed out the clear window to a black Cadillac that sat in the handicap parking space.

"Well sir, I can hold on while you get your wallet out the car," The cashier told him. She was chewing her gum like it was the last piece of gum on earth. Her hair had three different colors in it, and all I could smell was her fruity body spray.

"Oh, all right. I 'preciate that so kindly, ma'am." He grabbed his cane and took a couple of slow steps before turning his head and asking, "How much did you say that amount was again, dawlin'?"

"You need nine dollars and forty-two cents, sir," she answered, giving her gum three pops in a row.

"Okay, I have to go and get it. I can be back in here in no time," he announced, slowly moving toward the exit.

What was I supposed to do in the meantime, stand here and read the whole issue of Jet magazine? I had to go home and prep this food up before dad and his friends showed up. I reached into my pocket and pulled out the ten-dollar bill that Chris gave me in the car. It didn't matter to me. I had Chris's credit card to back me up.

"Excuse me sir, I can pay for your groceries." I said, passing the $10 bill to him. "Somebody blessed me with it and put that in my hands, so I think I should pass that blessing on to you," I explained.

He gave me a skeptical look from above his thick glasses.

"Are you giving this to me because you're in a rush, or did the Lord really put it in your heart?" He asked me.

"Somebody blessed me with it."

"I'll tell you like this," he added. "I can tell when someone gives from the heart. It's the unwholesome giving that I don't accept," he explained. "You can keep that money."

He turned toward the cashier. "Thank you, ma'am, for your patience."

"Oh, you're welcome sir."

The cashier looked at me like I stole candy from a baby, which made me feel belittled. I didn't mean any harm; I was just trying to help.

I went into the kitchen to check on the garlic bread. "The bread will be about five more minutes," I hollered. I grabbed the silverware and the big bowl of spaghetti and meatballs off of the kitchen counter, walked into the dining area, and passed them to Chris. "Your spaghetti came out looking good, too, Chris. I never tried it with Italian sausage before."

"I can put together a little sumfin-sumfin at times. I just got to be in the mood to cook, as you can see." After a brief pause, she added, "Why didn't you give Darren your phone number?"

"Because I know someone who is that sexy got a woman swinging off his arms somewhere," I said to her

"Yeah, but how would you know?"

"I don't know. But I do know that we would spend our first night out together seeing all his ex-girlfriends. "

"Don't let your assumptions block you from getting what you want."

"Girl, please. He wasn't my type anyway."

"Nick, you froze up. Y'all wouldn't have talked if I hadn't 've butted in," she told me sarcastically before entering the kitchen. She came out with our homemade punch with pineapples hanging around the rim of the bowl. She sat it down on the small coffee table in the corner along with the matching glasses. "I think you and him would look good together. I thought he was okay. Shoot, he tried to stop you from cussing, for goodness sake. Don't that tell you something?"

"I guess so," I admitted. "Oh well, it's too late now. If it was meant to be, we'll meet again."

"In the meantime you gone mess around and let yo' stuff close back up." She laughed, but I didn't join her. I didn't think that was funny. I was raped twice in my life—once by Harold and once by Ice-One. I don't know if I'm ready to open myself up to another man just yet.

After a few minutes, Chris went back into the kitchen and got the bread from the oven. The table was now set and the food was ready. We were now ready to have our guest over and enjoy the holiday.

I picked up the house phone and dialed Pop's cell phone:

"Hello," he answered.

"Hey pop, where y'all at?" I asked.

"We right at the complex; we just pulled into the parking lot. We had to go home and get cleaned up first. Is the food ready?"

"Talk about timing; we just pulled the last of the food from the oven."

"Okay, we'll be up shortly."

"Okay, see you."

.

Chris's cell phone rang. It was Daneena—one of Chris's childhood friends. Daneena is the only person I know who is our age and owns a Suburban, a BMW, and a house. All of them are paid off. Daneena gets anything she wants from her father. He is the owner of the hottest club in Detroit, which is called Midnight Tomorrow's. In order to get in, you have to either be VIPs or know somebody who knows somebody. Or just having a wad of cash would get you through. Last week, the club was in the newspaper as the top place to go to when you visit Detroit. When all the basketball players and the big ballers come to this city, that's where you'll find them. There are pool tables and bars with slot machines on one end of the club. And on the other side is where the party is at. There's a VIP room upstairs with a swimming pool and a sauna for the most expensive privacy you can imagine. Downstairs has little rooms to go in when you find that certain something you need. Those rooms cost just as much as a room at the Ramada Inn.

"Hello?" Chris answered. "Oh hey girl, what's hap'nin?…oh, we about to start serving the food now…you outside now?…well come on in, we just about got everything ready." Chris turned toward me and whispered, "Ain't yo' dad downstairs too?"

I pulled back the shade and looked out of the window. "Yeah, he's coming up the walkway now."

"Nina, do you see those three men in the parking lot? You can come on in with them and we'll buzz you up together…Okay, see ya," She said, and then she hung up.

"Dang Nick, I sure hope everything taste right," she said. "I know Nina is good for telling somebody that their cooking is trifling."

I don't care too much for Daneena. Something about her makes my skin crawl and the hairs on my neck stand up. But I put up with her just for Chris's sake.

I mumbled, "I bet she won't come up in here in my house talking all that yang-yang. Not today—little ugly heffa."

"Did you say something, Nick?"

"As a matter of fact, I did. But it's not repeatable," I answered.

One of these days, I will tell Chris how I really feel about Nina. She is the most arrogant person I have ever met. On top of that, I think she is gay. The way she looks at Chris's behind goes a little overboard at times. Plus, Ms. Drag Queen Diva got controlling issues. She think everyone should do what she says when she says it.

"Well if she didn't tell us what sucked, she wouldn't be Nina, now would she?" Chris said, trying to sound informal.

I scoffed. "I'll be right back. I gotta straighten up my make up and change this dirty shirt."

"And turn down the heat a little bit; it's kinda hot in here," She demanded while grabbing onto the front of her shirt and bouncing it against her chest.

I strutted to the mirror that hung on the living room wall and wiped the smudged lipstick from my chin. I opened the door.

"Hey, Pop."

"Move!" Daneena demanded. "Where is Chris?" she barged in through the door without an invitation and stormed into the kitchen area as I watched her crazy disposition.

"Hey, baby girl." Papa G hunched his shoulders and threw his arms around me. "It smell good up in here, and I'm starving," he said.

I gave Papa G and his friends hugs as they made their entrance.

"Hey y'all. Come on in," I softly spoke, and I shut the door.

"What did Chris do to her?" he whispered.

"It's what nature did to her that made her pissed." Tony, Phillip, Papa G, and I snickered. Nina didn't hear it. She was too busy running around the house trying to find Chris.

"Y'all can have a seat," I told them, grabbing the remote control and turning the TV on to a football game. The Giants and the Raiders were playing. "I'll be right back."

I crept toward the master bedroom to see where Nina went and why she was all up in our house like this. I put my ears up to the closed bedroom door just to hear what was going on. I heard nothing. I knocked. I still heard nothing. I tried to twist the door open, but it was locked. I backed away from the door and returned to the front room.

Pop dropped his chin and asked, "Is everything okay?"

I walked right past the mirror in the living room again and a caught reflection of the puzzled reaction on my face. I was so busy trying to figure out what they were up to that I didn't take their coats, nor did I offer them a drink.

"Shoot. I dunno. I refuse to let my Thanksgiving be spoiled."

"So when do we eat?" Tony asked.

"Just as soon as Chris and Daneena come back out," I said, walking toward the table.

All I could do was wonder what could be going on in the room. We waited for thirty minutes for Chris and Daneena. I knocked on the door again.

"Chris!" *Knock, knock, knock.* "Hello, Chris?" *Knock, knock, knock.* There was still no answer. I closed my eyes and took a deep breath to release the frustration. Then I went back into the dining room.

"Okay...um...I'm ready to eat when y'all are," I announced.

"Oh, yeah. I've been ready since yesterday," Tony said. He was the first one to jump to his feet. "Isn't Chris and whatchamacallit eating with us?"

"I have no idea," I said sarcastically. I washed my hands and took out a plate. I went for the macaroni and cheese spoon when Tony reached over the table and grabbed my hand.

"Shouldn't we say grace before we eat?"

I was still upset with Chris, and I shot Tony a look that might have burned a hole through his face if my looks were a laser gun.

"I'm sorry y'all. It's just that every time that girl pops up, something funny goes on," I said, pointing toward the room they were in.

Tony cleared his throat and then prayed for the food.

"Now Heavenly Father, we are gathered here today to give thanks for your blessing. Lord, you have blessed Christyl and Nicole with the energy and finances to prepare this food as well as you allowed us to be here together to enjoy it. Now, Lord, we ask that you bless those hands that prepared it and let this food give us nourishment for our bodys' sakes. Amen."

"Don't worry about it, honey. Whatever your friend is doing in there, that is her business."

I scoffed before taking the macaroni spoon from the bowl and helping myself.

"Yeah, and now it's everyone else's too," I said.

Chapter Twenty-three

"That Was Foul."

I woke up feeling tired. I got dressed and drove to work before Chris got out of the bed. When she arrived at work, she had a nonchalant look on her face that led me to believe something improper had happened in the bedroom, but she was mad at me for it. She wasn't dressed in her hotel uniform either. She had on the black soft cotton Rocawear jogging suit I bought her for her birthday. She stormed in, rolled her eyes at me, then marched to the restroom.

I sat behind the front desk doing the night audits. Victor, the arrogant-headed punk, hotel manager, came in. The only reason I deal with him is that he signs my checks. He is the cockiest person I know. On top of that, he is a womanizer who tries to get the goods every chance he gets. If he knows that there is something you want from him, he will have to get what he wants from you first. Even the Lexus he drives was paid off by his live-in girlfriend. That is why I never asked him to do me a favor. However in a weird sort of way, sometimes his cockiness is sexy and challenging.

"Nicole," he sung, "very nice to see you. You look nice today."

He walked up behind me and looked over my shoulder as if he was interested in the log book. He was so close I heard the air being inhaled and exhaled through his nostrils. I knew he wasn't interested in seeing the log book. He never is.

"Hi, Victor." I leaned to the side and turned around to face him. He jumped back.

"Is there something I can help you with?" I asked.

"Come to think of it…there is. I wanted to show you how much I appreciate your help. Lately you have really been working hard, coming to work on time, and not getting any write-ups." His eyes were scrolling up and down my backside while he spoke.

"I'm just doing my job, Victor," I said to him before returning my eyes to the log book. He stood behind me for a while in silence doing God knows what before he spoke again.

"Nicole, can I ask you a question?"

"It all depends," I answered.

"It depends on what?"

"On what your question is," I answered.

"Huh?"

"Never mind, Victor. What's your question?"

"Do you have any plans for Saturday?"

I looked up from my books dispassionately.

"I don't believe I have any plans, Victor. If you need me to cover for Heather while she goes to see her sick aunt, then it shouldn't be a problem."

"No, it's not that. I already found someone to replace her," he said.

"Okay, so why do you ask?"

"All I wanted to do was show you my appreciation. I want to take you out and buy you a dinner or a drink or something."

I took a deep breath. "So let me get this straight, you show your appreciation to your workers by getting them drunk? What happened to the old-fashioned way—buy a cake or print out an award?" I chuckled.

He rolled his eyes to the top of his head and smacked his teeth. "I'm serious, Nicole. I just want to treat you to a nice dinner or something. That's all."

"Okay, Victor, if it's strictly business, then it shouldn't hurt." I said, throwing him a look from the corners of my eyes.

"Of course it's not going to hurt—unless you go and order up a whole lotta stuff off the menu." He laughed, but I didn't join him. So he rephrased his answer. "Don't be silly. I'm not gon' do anything to harm you."

Chris walked out of the restroom and into the reception area. She came in when Victor was laughing. She smacked her teeth, tossing her backpack underneath the counter like she was upset.

"I'm sorry I'm late, Victor. The electricity in the building must have shut off the clock and knocked the time off track." She looked at me with her lips turned upward as if it was really my fault she was late.

"So wait a minute. Why is it that Nicole makes it here on time and you are just walking in?"

"I'm not Nicole, Victor," She said before clearing her throat as a sign of sarcasm.

"I can clearly see that." He looked at my behind and made a kissing noise. He walked to the copy machine and grabbed the faxes from it. "Just don't let it happen again, aight?" he commanded before opening the door to his office. He walked in and slammed the door behind him.

Chris threw her hands in my face. "And why in the hell you can't wake nobody up, bitch?" Chris sharply asked.

"You might want to take that hand out of my face. And watch your language."

"Or what?"

"Or you will catch a beat down." I slapped her hands away, rolled my eyes, focused my attention back on the log book, and began flipping the pages. "You and Daneena was rude, running in the back room doing God knows what."

"Wait a minute; hold up! Since when did that become any of your concern what Nina and I did in my own room? I pay rent there too, you know."

"You're right, it's not my concern what you and Nina do in the privacy of your room, Chris. I could care less. The thing that bothered me was her barging in the door, being rude. Then she goes into the back room and stays with you for thirty minutes. I didn't like that. That wasn't cool at all," I said to her.

"I don't see where it's a big deal. That was all your family out there, not mine."

"So you went through all the trouble cooking and cleaning up for me and my people?" I stepped off the stool and got closer to her face.

My voice dropped into a smoother tone. "That's really nice of you, Chris. However, the next time you and Nina decide to eat something else for Thanksgiving dinner, I wish you'd let me know."

"Whatever, Nick. You don't know what went on in my room, so keep your nose to yourself. And move up out my face; yo' breath stank," she demanded.

"The hell with my breath. I'm tired of playin' these games with you, Chris. What is it about this girl that gets you so nervous? Do you see how she's running your life? I think you scared of her or something, aren't you?" I sat back down on my barstool without my eyes leaving her face.

"Scared?"

"Yes, scared."

"Well who died and made you my watcher? You wasn't shit when I met you, so who are you to judge me?"

"Oh I wasn't shit, huh?"

"Yeah, I said it. I heard you and Victor making plans to go out to dinner. All laughin' and heeheeing. I hope he don't do you like he did me."

"And exactly what is it that he did to you?" I asked Chris.

Victor's entrance into the room startled both of us. He came out of his office, rudely interrupting my question.

"Oh, Nicole. I forgot to tell you 8:00 p.m. at Midnight Tomorrow's. You know where it's at, right?"

"Yeah, I know exactly where it is." I looked at Chris and then at Victor. "I'll see you at eight o'clock."

Chris looked at him with disgust before letting out a scoff. She slammed the stapler on the desk, grabbed the stack of credit card receipts from her side of the counter, and marched to the back of the reception area where the file cabinets were.

I felt like whupping Christyl's ass. Any other time I would have been more concerned about her feelings, but this time I didn't care.

I looked at Victor and shrugged my shoulders. I could tell he was curious. He looked like he was excited to see two females arguing. "What was that all about?" he asked with a huge smile on his face.

I looked at him and frowned. "It was about getting in each other's business. Now do you mind?"

Chapter Twenty-four

"The Promotion"

While it was still partially frozen in the middle, I took the lasagna from the oven—along with some garlic bread—placed them on the table, and sat down.

"God is good, God is great. Thank you, Lord, for the food… Amen."

When I was done eating, I looked up at the clock and realized what I had just done. It took me forty-five minutes to cook a partially frozen Lasagna and only three minutes to scarf it down. I knew I was going to pay for that sometime today.

I went into my closet and pulled out my favorite red, stiletto-heeled, pointy-toed shoes. I looked into the cabinet of purses and pulled out my matching red Versace handbag.

My red-and-silver halter top would accent my waistline just right. I think I'll wear that one, I thought.

I took the halter out of the Macarthur Cleaners bag, inspected it, and laid it across the bed. *That old, faithful, favorite pair of denim, boy-cut, low-riding jeans of mine would look good with this.* I searched and searched the room, but couldn't find them. That's when I remembered that Chris wore them, spilled a margarita on them, and took them to the cleaners.

I reached inside the closet and pulled out a different pair of faithful lowriders and slid them on my body. They weren't the ones that accented my backside the way I wanted them to, but they would have to do for now.

As I sat at the vanity mirror getting ready to apply my make up, the vibration of Chris's cellular phone startled me.

"That's odd," I thought. "She never leaves home without it."

With my braless breasts dancing across the stage of my chest, I ran to the kitchen and snapped it from the charger cord.

"It's Daneena," I mumbled. I held Christyl's cell phone in my hand, wondering if I should answer it or leave it alone. Daneena hung up the phone. "Good. Who on earth wants to talk to her anyway?"

She called back before I could step one foot back into my room. I thought that maybe Chris could be with Daneena andwas looking for her cell phone. I pressed the call button and put it to my ear.

"Chris, where have you been?" Daneena asked before I could greet her with a hello. "And tell me what could be so important that you can't answer your phone when I call?"

"Humph," I mumbled before she continued.

"I thought I told you to call me when you got home. What happened to you?" she asked.

"Daneena?" I said with class.

"What?"

"Chris left her phone at the house," I said to her.

"Where is she?"

"I don't know where she is."

She scoffed. "Don't y'all work together?"

"Yes, we do," I answered.

"When you see her, tell her I'm on the way to the club. If she still want the sack, she'll find me down there."

"So now you want me to do you a favor," I said out of sarcasm. "What kind of sack are you talking about?"

Daneena paused. Before she spoke, she cleared her throat. "Just give her the message for me, will you. Thank you." She said, and then she hung up.

At the club, huh? What a coincidence, that is where I'm headed. I hope she doesn't start trouble. We wouldn't want to have an ambulance and a police squad car parked along the walkway like I did back in high school, now would we?

Vic called my cell phone five minutes before I arrived at the club's parking garage. He told me that he would be waiting for me outside the door. I still had access to get into the club by myself, even though Nina and I didn't get along. I told him to go in and wait for me at the bar area. Unfortunately, he didn't take my advice.

"Yo, Nick—over here," he yelled through a line of people who were standing around while trying to get in.

I took my time strutting in my stilettos. I wasn't going to let him rush me into falling. Then he got louder.

"Yo! Nick!" He waved his hands.

I thought I told him to meet me at the bar. Men can be hardheaded at times.

I took my time walking. In the line was my girl Tonya, my mother's hairdresser; Timmara, a good friend from middle school; Vanessa, the cashier from the grocery store; And the light-skinned brother down the street named Jonathon. I took three minutes of my time to talk to him. Why not? He was my friends too.

By the time I got to Victor, his mood was pesky. His facial expression was overflowing with frustration.

"Are you done?" he asked. His reaction to my friendliness let me know that he was feeling unappreciated. I thought that was cute.

"Just because you are my boss at the job doesn't mean that you are the boss of my life," I said.

"Okay. I hear you," he said. He took my hand and led me into the club.

Inside it wasn't as busy as it was on the weekends. Victor and I sat at the bar and ordered our drinks. He ordered a Heineken, while I courageously ordered a margarita. Vic lit up a cigarette and took a puff.

"Ms. Popularity."

"Who, me?"

"Yes, you."

"I'm not that popular; Those were just friends I socialize with."

"Friends you socialize with, huh?" he took a drag of his cigarette and blew the smoke out of his mouth forcefully. "Mr. Yellow Man didn't seem like that to me. He was all up on yo' stuff."

"One of them was from school; the other, work; and one is a hairdresser. Why the hell are you checking me like you my man?"

"I am not trying to check you. I'm just trying to peep your style. That's all," he said, taking another puff of his cigarette.

"Um, Victor?"

"Yeah."

"Can I ask you a question?"

"Go ahead," he answered.

Victor reclined in his barstool. He propped his Timberlain boots upon the footrest of my barstool and placed his knees between my legs.

"Am I here for appreciation, or to get checked?"

He took another hit of his cigarette. This time he inhaled with more force and exhaled the smoke as he spoke. "Answer this, Nicole: how come a pretty young thang like you don't have a man in her life?"

"I don't have time for all the game playing. I'm not real fond of my time being wasted on the bull that men put us through," I answered, sipping on my tropical drink.

His cigarette was tempting. I gave Victor a nod as a sign for him to pass me one of his Newports. He took one out of the green box and passed it to me. I put it to my lips. He lit the tip of my cigarette with his dice-shaped lighter, which he then tucked into his pocket. On his wrist, I could smell the same cologne Mike wore the day he died—Paco Rabanne.

"Here, you might want another one," He said, sliding the box of cancer sticks across the bar.

"Oh, naw. I'm cool," I said, sliding the box back across the bar. "I smoke every now and then."

"Well, take one anyway. You might want one later on or something." He took one out of the box and passed it to me. I grabbed the cigarette from his hand and placed it in my purse.

"Women play games too. I don't know why it's always us men that seem to be the problem," he said.

"You're right. There are lots of women who play games. I just know that I'm not ready to take on the drama that comes along with having a relationship. I like being single."

I looked up and saw Daneena walking in our direction. I took another drag of my cigarette and warned Victor of Daneena's arrival.

As he looked upon her approach, his facial expressions had shown signs of disapproval.

"I hope she don't come over here," he said.

"I hope she don't come over here talking shit."

Daneena walked up to Victor, extending her palm out for a handshake. Victor shifted in his barstool.

"Well hello there," she sung. "I think I saw you before, but we haven't been properly introduced. I'm Daneena, and you are...?"

Victor did not extend his hand. His look told me that their last encounter wasn't a very pleasant one. "I am who I am," he said before focusing his attention back on his drink.

"Hey Gary, can I have another one of these?" Victor asked Gary, the bartender. Gary was so into the Pistons playoff game that he didn't hear Victor's request.

"Gary...Dawg...can I get another hookup, big baby?"

"My bad, playa." The slim bartender scurried to retrieve Victor's drink. He popped the top, slid it in front of him, and then went back to watching his game.

Nina cleared her throat. "Gary, you can make that one on the house. I'm sure my dad wouldn't mind."

Victor spun around in his chair. "Your dad, huh?"

"Oh, you didn't know?"

"Know what?" Victor asked.

"That my dad owns the club?" Her smile showed enticement, but Victor's face showed rejection.

Victor spun around in his barstool. "What did you say your name was? Daneena, right?"

She smiled from ear to ear. "Yes...it's Daneena."

"Okay, Daneena. No thanks, I can pay for my own drinks,"

"Well, it's a lot better when you *don't* have to pay for it, isn't it?" Nina remarked.

Too bad she had no clue that her presence had once again become an annoyance. I cleared my throat. "What do you want Nina?"

"I saw you guys from up there." she said while pointing to the luxurious second floor office suite. "Just thought I'd come over and say hello, see how everything's going, and meet your new friend, Nicole."

She looked at him with her seductive eyes. Vic grabbed his drink from the counter and paid no attention to her advances.

"Daneena,you still don't have a clue, do you?" I asked.

"A clue about what?" Daneena asked.

I scoffed. "That's exactly what I thought."

I turned my back to her and placed my manicured hands on the glass of my tropical drink.

"Well, it was a pleasure seeing you both. And I hope to see you around again." She grabbed a pretzel from the bar and put it in her mouth, licking her fingers. Victor still showed no signs of impression. He was to busy looking like he had a case of bad indigestion. Danena winked her eyes before walking away.

"You know who that is?" Vic asked, holding his stomach with one hand and placing the other on his forehead.

"Yeah, that's one of Chris's ugly friends. She used to stay on Chris's street or something like that. She's the one who's been making her late for work for the past month," I told him.

Victor picked up his drink and gulped it down. After slamming the empty bottle onto the bar, he sat and stared at me as if he wanted to say something.

"Victor, why are you looking at me like that?" I chuckled. "You look like a diablo from Garbon?"

"Forget that Nicole. If I tell you something, you promise you won't say shit to anybody?"

"It's safe," I said confidently.

"I want to ask you about your girl. I mean, is she aight in the head?"

"Daneena or Chris?"

"I'm not talking about Neena. I'm talking about your girl Christyl."

"What do you mean 'is she all right'? All right like what?"

"You promise you won't say anything, right?"

"Vic, would you just come out and say it? We've been through the scouts honor shit already," I told him.

"Well, I'm sure you know by now that I have been banging your girl on the low-low, and—"

"No, she hasn't told me that part yet, but go ahead," I interrupted.

"One minute we're cool, then the next minute she's brushing me off."

"Go on."

"Well, she start doing things really strange—coming in late for work, acting all secretive, dressing different. Just seem suspicious to me."

"And?" I sat back nonchalantly as I sipped on my tropical drink.

"Finally, she came around apologizing to me, along with the hopes of starting a relationship."

I nodded.

"Well, When I told her I could no longer be with her and that I was going to marry, Daniece, she went on and on about how tired she was of men. She said that none of us are any good and that she won't be able to find a man good enough for her. I thought she was kidding until one day I popped up at your house."

"My house."

"Yes, your house. You were gone somewhere with your father."

"Okay, go on."

"Well, I knocked on the door and Chris opened it. She was butt naked and full of sweat."

"Maybe she was in the shower."

"Or maybe she wasn't."

"What's your point, Vic?" I said, picking up my drink again and taking another sip. "I'm getting bored."

"Her hair was all over the place. And plus, who wraps a sheet around them when they come outta the shower?"

"So what! Maybe she was fucking somebody else other than you, big deal. What are you trying to say, Vic?"

"I think your girl is gay."

I sat back in my chair and took a deep breath. I already knew about Chris and Nina's little cat scannings, but I just played it off.

"So why would you think she's gay? What gave you the impression that a woman was in the room?"

"Well, I wanted to come in and talk to her about the situation with me and Daniece. Hell, Chris and I still gotta work at the hotel together, right?"

"Right," I answered.

"And I didn't want any static between us when we came back to work on Monday. I just wanted to make sure that we had an understanding so she won't blow a fuse at the job."

"Go on," I said

"Nina was in Chris's room, Nicole. Your girl is a freak." He started to laugh, but he saw that I wasn't laughing with him, so he stopped. "I barged in, went to the back room and saw that girl, Nina, lying naked in the bed."

"And what happened after that?"

"I called both of them nasty and walked out."

"Damn!" I uttered.

"Hell, I like Christyl. I was going to offer her the assistant manager position until I realized she was unable to keep up with the standards. How can she help run a office when her mind is being controlled by somebody else? It's almost like this girl Nina has her under a spell."

I knew something was up with Chrystal and Victor. That's what Chris meant by "I hope he don't do you like he did me." Victor turned her into a bisexual.

"So the assistant manager position is mine?" I asked. I didn't care about Chrystal or Nina anymore; I was tired of hearing about them. All I knew was that Nicole had to take care of Nicole.

"If you want it," he answered, "it's yours."

"You have yourself an assistant manager." I told him, extending my hand out for a handshake.

He took my hand into his and kissed it. I became weak for love that night. Victor showed me the size of his manhood. We got drunk and ended up together on his couch the next morning. Naked.

Chapter Twenty-five

"The Correction."

"Where is she?" Daneena barged into my office with her hands on her hips.

"Excuse you, Daneena; shouldn't you knock first?" I said to her. "Who do you think you are?"

I was sitting at my office desk looking over the inventory listing for the housekeepers when she walked in. Daneena was upset. Almost like someone had just stolen her car, or better yet, like her father had told her that she couldn't have any of his fortunes anymore.

"I thought that I told you to call me when Chrystal comes back," she answered. " I know that she is around here somewhere."

I rose to my feet. It was obvious that she needed a reality check. Did she really think that I was going to let her come into my office and talk to me this way? Was she crazy?

"Look here Nina, as long as I have been coming into your club, I have never came in and disrespected you like this at your place of business," I said to her just as calmly as I would talk to a newborn baby.

"I don't care if you did. I got niggas in there that would blow your ass to pieces if you stepped up to me. Do you think I'm worried about you?"

Now that did it. She blew the last bit of patience I had for her ugly ass.

"No, but you will be in a minute. Stay right there." I had on some dress slacks with stilettos and a collared shirt. I stepped on the back heels of my shoes, kicking them to the side of my desk. This was my opportunity to whup her ass. I was going to make sure that this was the last time she talked shit to me.

I scooted my chair back and jumped to my feet. "You have about two minutes to haul ass up outta here, before I—"

"Before what? What you gon' do to me? You don't have any guts, you yellow bitch."

"Like hell if I do," I told her. "For a struck-match-looking-ass villain, you sure talk a lot of shit."

"Whatever. Where's Chris?" she asked.

"One and a half minutes." I looked at my wristwatch before pressing the call button for some security. David, from valet parking answered.

"Yes Ms. Lewis."

"David call an ambulance, 'cause I'm dearly about to whup somebody's ass."

"Are you serious?" David asked in surprise, but I didn't respond.

"Come on," I threw up my fists and stood in fighting position. "Bring it on, Bitch. I have been waiting for this moment since you started talking shit the first time."

"Bitch, please, you don't know me." Daneena took her shoes from her raggedy, pedicured feet and began walking toward me.

I jumped forward, cocked my arm back, and *wham*!

Daneena hit the floor after she fell into Victor's desk.

"I told you not to come in here like that didn't I?"

Daneena wiped her jaw. "You have no idea what you just did, do you?"

"Oh, I see you still here. Didn't I tell you that you had one minute to get out of here?"

David walked in while I was cocking my fist back again. He came in with two other drivers, Cedric and Phoenix.

"Ms. Lewis, wait!" Cedric shouted. Phoenix ran over to help Daneena up from the floor. David grabbed my arms and began rubbing my back to calm me down from all the hype.

Daneena rose to her feet and ran toward me. Before I could realize that this animal broke free from Phoenix's strong hold, she let me have it.

"*Wham!*"

In the back of my head, I felt a sharp pain. Daneena's fist was the last thing I wanted to feel upside my head.

I picked up the guest chair and tossed it across the room, trying to knock her to the floor again. Phoenix and Cedric jumped to the side, but David tried to catch the chair. The legs swiped across his face before landing on Daneena. And just like I had wanted, Daneena hit the floor again.

I ran up to her while she lay panting and helplessly crying for forgiveness. I smacked, punched, and kicked her until I realized she gave in. I was the champ and this was my office. I tried to tell her, but she didn't listen.

"I told y'all to call the ambulance."

Chapter Twenty-six

"Pulling the Strings"

"Dang, Chris. What happened to you?"

For the early part of the day, it was sunny and warm. But suddenly, the dark clouds grew thick. And for the last two hours it had been raining nonstop. Chris walked in. Her deep-waved hair weave had been drenched with the rain, and her clothes were soaking wet. She had a duffle bag strapped across her shoulders and a lit joint in her hand. This was odd. Chris had been gone for a whole month without a sign as to where she had been, and finally she came back looking like a lost puppy.

Where had she been? Why was her lover trying to find her? And why was Victor so angry that he came to a point where firing her was the only option? I had to find out.

"I thought you'd be the last one to be concerned about me," with her head down. She tossed her keys on the coffee table and dropped her bag onto the floor. She plopped down on the couch, clapping her hands over her face.

"I don't know why you would say that. You know that I care about you," I said to her.

Chris shrugged her shoulders. "I don't know; I'm just confused."

"Confused about what?" I asked sincerely.

"Never mind…it's nothing."

Now I was confused. I knew she was high and all, but damn.

She threw her head back against the couch and released a long sigh. "I left my cell phone here; have you seen it?" Chris asked.

"Yeah, I did. Let me go get it." I walked out of the living room and into the bedroom feeling puzzled as hell. I was hoping she would help me see the light of all that had been going on with her.

I grabbed her cell phone from the nightstand in my room and walked back into the living room. I placed the cell phone in her hands. "I cut it off so all your calls could go straight to your voicemail."

"Thank you," Chris said. She took hold of the phone, flipped it open, and turned it on. Her mood was content, and her tone was mellow. She showed no emotion as she dialed her voicemail and listened.

"I was about to make myself some hot tea; would you like some?" I asked, walking into the kitchen.

Chris took the phone from her ears and gave me a nod.

I took another mug and saucer from the cupboard and placed it on the counter. As the water began whistling in the kettle, I slowly stirred the hot water into mugs with tea bags in them. I grabbed an ashtray and the tea cups and placed them on the dining room table.

"Thank you," she obliged. She stood up from the couch, walked over to the table, sat down in the chair, and dumped her joint ashes into the ashtray. While continuously listening to her messages, she stirred her hot tea.

"You're welcome," I responded.

The room was still and silent except for the woman's voice that echoed from her cell phone's earpiece. Chris would not look into my face. Her face had no expression as she threw her head back and scoffed. "I hate her," she announced.

"Hate who?" I curiously asked.

She didn't answer. Chris pressed a number on her phone to listen to the next message. This time I could recognize that it was a man's voice.

"Hate who, Chris?" I asked again, but she gave me no response.

Since she did not bother to answer, I stirred my tea and waited patiently for her to finish her phone call, hoping she would explain everything when it ended.

"Oh no he didn't!" she said, shaking her head and slamming the hand that was holding the joint, against the table.

At that point I realized that whatever it was, it wasn't my business to know. If only I could hear clearly what the messages on her phone were about, I could figure this whole thing out by myself.

Biting her lips, she pressed another button to retrieve the next message. This time, I could clearly hear who it was. It was Darlene shouting from the top of her lungs.

"Chrystal Manning! When you get this message, you call me. I got a bone to pick with you!" she said, and then she slammed the phone on the hook.

Chris flipped the phone shut and placed it on the table. She took a long drag of the joint and held it. With the teaspoon in the other hand, she began stirring in a soft and delicate motion. Finally she looked into my eyes and leaned back in her chair, blowing the smoke into the air.

While I quietly sipped on my tea, I could hear her short, quick breaths entering and exiting her nostrils.

"You want to talk about it?" I asked.

She took a deep breath. "I don't know Nick. I can't explain it right now," she finally said.

"Why?"

Chris smacked her teeth. "I just can't."

I leaned back in my chair, having visions of myself jumping up and putting my hand around her little neck. She was starting to irk me. My patience was running thin and I couldn't take it anymore.

"Um-kay," I said. I grabbed my tea and headed toward my bedroom.

"Wait Nick!" she calmly demanded. She sprung up from her seat and grabbed my arm. "Please...sit."

I sat back in the chair and laid my mug on the table.

"I left because I had to get away from Daneena." She took another drag of her joint and held the smoke in her throat. "Her and I had some issues."

"Issues?"

"Yeah...issues." She chuckled and stared into her mug. "It was more like possessive issues."

"What did she do this time?" I asked.

"Well I don't want to go into details, but…can you believe she threatened me? She demanded that I quit my job because she didn't like me working with you."

"Are you serious?"

"Dead serious," she answered. "I told her that I ain't like that idea. Not one bit."

"Did you really?" I asked.

"I sure did. You have been my dawg from day one. Plus, I couldn't quit my job; I have too many bills to pay." She took a deep breath before she continued. "Victor was the only person I told. He was the only one that knew I was going out of town. Only because he was my boss and he understood that I was trying to get out of the mistake of becoming a lesbian."

"So have you recovered?" I asked.

"Recovered?" she asked curiously. "Recovered from what?"

"From being a lesbian?"

"I wasn't a lesbo to begin with," she answered, sipping on her tea. "I didn't want to mess around with her in the first place. She threatened me to do that too."

"Well I hope you don't start looking at me funny, 'cause I'm letting you know now that I don't play that." I bluntly told her.

Her lips parted into a smile "You won't have to worry about me wanting you in that way, Nicole. Even if I was gay, you not my type," she said while mashing the lit end into the ashtray. "But you and I might have to find somewhere else to stay," she insisted.

"I'm not running from Daneena. I doubt it if she come in here again."

Chris smiled widely, pulling her long hair behind her ear. "So this means you still got my back?"

"Oh yeah," I said to her. "I whooped dat ass in the office. Let her come on."

Chris chuckled. "You did what?"

"She came into the office talking shit. I took off my stilettos and let her have it. She was on the floor screaming for her life."

"Nick, did you put her in an ambulance?"

"Yes I did," I answered. "I told Phoenix and David to drag her ass outside the door so she can have closer access to the ambulance. I put her in her place real fast."

Chris laughed uncontrollably. She laughed so hard her eyes became teary. "I hope it's on video tape. I can't wait to see it."

"I took it out of the VCR and changed the tape after it happened. The original copy is in my desk."

We both laughed.

"So do you forgive me?" Chris asked.

"I never had anything against you," I answered.

"So will you give me my job back, Ms. Manager of the Year?"

"I should be able to pull some strings."

We stood up together and threw our arms around one another. She was the best friend I have ever had. And no matter what mistake she made, I had to have her back.

Chapter Twenty-seven

"Tough Situation."

It was Friday afternoon; the hotel was busy. Chris and I had been working since five o'clock this morning. It was now two o'clock in the afternoon and our spaghetti dinners were waiting for us in the hotel cafeteria's refrigerator. Chris started working in the housekeeping department. She decided to clean rooms instead of being anywhere near the office with Victor. After I finished my work, I grabbed my office keys, locked the door, and walked to the cafeteria. Chris was standing in front of the microwave and fanning herself with an empty paper plate.

"How long you been in here?" I asked.

"Five minutes," she said. "Why is it so hot in here?"

"What is up with you and these hot flashes, Chris?" I asked.

"I have no idea. I hope I'm not pregnant," she answered.

"That's funny you say that," I replied, "because I just might be."

Chris froze. Her eyes bulged from their sockets as if she'd just seen Christopher Reeves do a handstand. "Might be what? Pregnant! I knew your throwing up wasn't just from my cooking."

"My period hasn't shown up in two months, and Victor claims it's not his fault," I told Chris.

"Victor?" she exclaimed. "What the hell happened since I was gone?"

"I became a victim," I courageously confessed. "But that's what I get for being weak."

"You are not weak, Nicole. Victor just have his way of getting what he wants. And plus, the size of his gun would make any woman want to take a bullet."

"You so silly," I said.

We both laughed in unison, even though we knew that the situation was not comical.

"How do you feel about that, Chris?"

"Feel about what?"

"Me and Vic?"

"You my dawg. I'm here to support you. To hell with him," she bluntly exerted.

I grabbed my container from the refrigerator, placed it on the counter, and sat down. Chris took her dinner out of the microwave, grabbed my container, placed it in the microwave, and set it for five minutes.

"Chris?"

"Yeah."

"Could you go to the doctor with me? Just to find out the truth?"

"You know I will. Let's go now; they close at four," Chris said. "But what about Victor?"

"Fuck Victor," I answered. "It's his fault I'm in this predicament."

I looked at Chris in surprise, and she looked at me in shock. "Wait a minute, Chris; how do you know they close at four?"

"Don't even ask." She chuckled.

After we ate lunch, I returned to the office to pick up my purse, forward all my calls, and turn off the desk lamp.

"Nicole, where are you going?" Victor asked in surprise.

"I'm going home; I don't feel so good," I answered.

"You can't leave now. I thought you were going to do the credit card balances for me," Victor announced.

"I can't do them now, Victor; I feel sick."

Victor looked above his Pierre Cardin eyeglasses. "Those receipts have been sitting on your desk all morning. If they are on your desk, it means that you are supposed to do them."

"I am sorry. I was so swamped doing my own work that I didn't have time to do yours. Just wait until the midnight shift comes; they'll do it for you. It don't have to be turned in until tomorrow anyway."

"I don't want the midnight shift to do it; I told you to do it," he said. His voice boomed, but it didn't frighten me one bit. "I think you better sit over there and get this done before I write you up."

"What in the hell is your problem, Victor?" I asked. "You ain't got to get all nasty with me."

Victor rolled his eyes before rising to his feet. "Do them before you leave, Ms. Lewis," He said, and then he stormed out of the office door, leaving a trail of his cheap cologne behind.

"Ms. Lewis," I said to myself. "He wasn't calling me that when he was dripping sweat in my face, was he?"

I glanced over at Victor and his wife's wedding picture. I'd been staring at this photo on his desk for the last two weeks, and I was ready to throw it out of the window. What right did he have to put his and Daniece's wedding picture in the sterling silver frame I bought him for his birthday? Cheap-ass wannabe thug.

I opened Victor's desk drawer to look for his extra pack of cigarettes. I took two out just in case Chris wanted one and put the box back into the drawer. I grabbed my keys, purse, and sunglasses and strutted through the rotating doors without looking back or speaking to the customers who were coming in.

I said a silent prayer on the way to the car: *Nothing goes good in my life; I struggle day after day just to keep my head above water, but I only sink deeper. God, if it's your will, fix my life.*

Chris ran up behind me and jumped into the car. Her facial expression was telling me that she knew Victor had somehow pushed my buttons.

"It's fine, Nick. I'm here with you."

"I'm cool," I said. "I just hope the tests come out in my favor."

I swerved from lane to lane as I drove down the freeway. As the other drivers cleared my path, Chris shifted in her seat. My nerves were shot. I knew that if this technician said that I was pregnant, I was going to completely lose it. It wasn't long before a police squad car pulled up behind me, flashing its lights.

"Damn, Nick. The police is behind us," Chris informed me. "You might as well exit the ramp and pull over."

I said nothing. I pulled up the freeway ramp and into a service station and then put the car in park.

"Damn, I hope this don't take long." I said to Chris. "I wish I could tell him that I am just having a bad day and that I won't speed again."

I took one of the Newports out of my purse and lit the end before he reached the side of my car door.

"Hello, Nicole."

I looked into the officer's face, and to my surprise, it was Darren. My eyebrows lifted as I shifted uncomfortably in my seat.

"You don't remember me, do you?" he asked.

"Yes, I do remember you, Darren," I said politely. "How have you been?"

"Good. And you?" he answered. "I told you we would see each other again."

"Yeah, you did." Boy was I happy that it was him. At least I knew that I wouldn't be getting a ticket today.

Chris ducked her head down and waved her palm. "How ya doing there, Darren?"

"Oh, hello," he said to Chris. "Chris, right?"

"Yes…Chris." she sat back in her seat, placing one leg over another.

"Where are you ladies on your way to going so fast? You shouldn't be driving like that."

Chris and I looked at each other, wondering which one of us could come up with the best excuse. We both knew that we couldn't tell him where we were really on our way to. He continued. "You were swerving from one lane to the other. Some other officer would have given you a ticket."

"Oh yeah, I know," I said, biting my lip. I clutched onto the steering wheel as tightly as my hands would allow. I wanted to get to the doctor before they closed, so I had to think of something quick.

"Well, I appreciate you not giving me a ticket."

"No problem." He stared into my eyes as if he knew I was up to something. "Step out of the car, Nicole, so I can see you better."

I took a deep breath and blew it out effortlessly. I looked over at Chris. Chris's eyebrows lifted. An air bubble was forming in my stomach. I farted silently, leaving poor Chris to smell the aftershocks of the spaghetti dinner I just ate.

I got out of the car.

The aura between Darren and me was passive. He stood with humility, watching my shaking hands lift to take another drag of my cigarette. He grabbed the cigarette from my hand and stared at it.

"What are you doing with this?" His tone of voice was gentle. It tenderized the stiffness in the air. If I had known it was him driving the police car, I wouldn't have lit the cigarette in the first place.

"Smoking it."

"Do you know how pretty your lips are? Why are you abusing them?"

My head dropped immediately. I was too ashamed to look into his eyes. He was so sexy and looked so good in his uniform that I couldn't resist. "Darren?"

"What?"

"You look good… I mean damn good," I said to him, tucking my bottom lip between my teeth. My lips parted into a smile.

"You do too," he said. "If you're not busy later on, and when you clear the smoke from your breath, I could come over and—"

"Okay," I said before he could get his words out. just then, I remembered that I needed medical attention first. "How about I call you?"

"That sounds good," he answered.

Chris cleared her throat.

"Well, since you're not giving me a ticket or arresting me, can I go?"

"Okay," he agreed. "Would you at least take my number down and call me when you think it's the right time?"

"I guess so," I replied. While I nervously searched through the pocket of my slacks, my mobile phone dropped and hit the concrete. Luckily, it didn't break. Darren picked up my phone, brushed it off, and handed it back to me.

"Okay, what's the number?" I asked him.

"Wait…why don't I put my phone number in your phone for you." He pulled it from my nervous hands and entered his number. Now I was staring into his gorgeous face. He looked good in a uniform. His beard and hair were neatly trimmed, and he smelled damn good—and quite succulent, I might add.

God bless this child. Hallelujah! Thank you, Jesus!

"You do plan on calling me, right?" he sincerely asked, placing the phone back into my hands.

"Um, yeah I'll call you." He leaned over, trying to kiss my cheek. I leaned toward him too, but I jerked away before our lips touched.

"You are on duty, remember?"

"Yeah…too bad, ain't it?"

Silence filled the air.

"Bye, Darren," my lips whispered.

"See you soon, Nicole," he replied.

I drove out of the gas station and onto the road, feeling nauseated. I liked Darren a whole lot, but I might be pregnant by Victor the fixer. Bad timing? That's what I thought.

Chris looked at me and smiled. "Tough situation."

I looked at her and nodded my head. "Yeah, tough situation. But everything that happens in my life is in the nick of time. Just watch."

Chapter Twenty-eight

"In God We Trust."

If I'm not sitting on this toilet taking a piss or a dump, I'm finding my face lodged in it. There's no other way to explain morning sickness except by saying it's sickening. The way a pregnant woman needs her toilet bowl is the same way a man with halitosis needs a breath mint. It's a must have.

Chris stayed over at her mother's house, and Victor ended up spending the night at my apartment to discuss the plans of my pregnancy. The only problem was that after we were done, he was taking a shower as soon as I had to puke. I marched to the toilet bowl. It was then that I told him I was pregnant.

"So why not just get an abortion, Nicole?" Victor asked as he turned off the water valve from the shower. He stepped out of the tub and grabbed his towel. He began drying himself off.

I rose to my feet, washed my hands, and dried them with a hanging towel. I leaned forward against the sink, staring into the mirror and thinking about how the wild one-hour love encounter made me feel more guilty. I watched the reflection of his masculinity rise again, hoping it wasn't a gesture for round two because this time I just wasn't feeling it.

"Because I don't think it's right, Vic. I mean, I had an abortion when I was thirteen, and I don't want to do this again."

"If you know that having this baby will not change things between me and Daniece, why are you going through with this?"

"It's not about you or Daniece. It's about me making the right choices."

"Oh, now you decide to want to make a good choice. How come you didn't do it before?" he asked.

He wrapped his towel around his waist and leaned his rock-hard body against mine. His nature was rubbing on the crack of my butt, which made me feel more nauseated.

"Vic, get off of me," I demanded, pushing him away.

He grabbed my arms tight, spun me around, and forced me to look into his eyes. His tone became stern.

"Now you listen to me. I am going to call my cousin, Atria. Atria is going with you to make sure you unplug this bastard from your uterus. You call me and let me know when you get this over with. Take a few sick days off and come back to work like you normally do. Aight?"

Staring at him with despair, I snatched my arm from his lock and pushed him off. I walked out of the bathroom and into my bedroom. I slammed the door and plopped down on the bed. I began crying.

"He can't make me do this. This is my body, not his. It's not his choice."

His idea of taking care of things is waving money around and telling someone to get rid of it. He gave me one thousand dollars and gave Atria my cell phone number. I prayed before I made my appointment.

At the clinic, I did just the opposite. When I spoke to the counselors, they convinced me not to go through with the surgery if I wasn't 100 percent sure of what I wanted to do. I agreed. I grabbed my purse and the hand of Victor's nineteen-year-old cousin and walked out of the building. How dare he send me with a nineteen year old. What is this teaching her?

Victor wasn't very pleased with that decision, but who cares. I wasn't very pleased with him either. So now we're even. Even though Victor told Atria to make sure I went along with the surgery, she was the one trying to convince me to keep the baby.

Over the next several months, Atria became like a little sister to me. I reached my fifth month and she was still standing by my side. She came over after I got off of work just to make sure I was eating properly and getting enough rest. She was there through the crying spells, the aches and pains, and the engaging ceremonies during which I had to put my whole face in the toilet bowl. What a sight to let someone else see.

"Do you need anything else, Nick?" Atria asked, peeking her head inside the bathroom door with a glass of salt water in her hand.

"No, sweetie, I'm fine. I'll just gargle with the salt water to help take this God-forsaken vomit taste from my mouth." I was trying to stand on my feet, but I was too weak.

Atria placed the salt water on the sink and rushed over to my aid. "Should I stick around for a while just in case you need anything?"

"Uh-uh, girl. You don't need to stay here and watch me throw up all day," I said to Atria. "You have a class to go to, and I don't want to keep you from it."

"I can always get the notes from somebody. It's not like I have a test to take."

"If you want to stay, Atria, you can stay. But I don't want you to mess up your studies," I said. I picked up the salt water from the bathroom counter and started gargling.

Atria had two brothers who were serving time in the marines. She had no sisters, and a lot of her cousins were either too old and had kids or were to young to be on her social level. So in her eyes, I'm the big sister and cousin she never had. For the past three months, She had been bringing her homework to my house and studying until her head dropped onto her books. I must admit, I like the fact that someone is looking up to me like this. And just like she encouraged me to have this baby, I encouraged her to continue her education and sign up for college courses.

"Thanks, Nick. I promise I'm not messing up my studies. I got it under control. Don't worry about me; you got enough stuff to worry about."

I spit the water into the face bowl. "Yeah, and you have enough to worry about too. You have the opportunity to attend college; that's why

I'm making sure somebody worries about it." I took another mouthful of salt water and swished it around.

"I know, I know…but trust me, I'm not missing anything in class today—just a lecture. And plus it'll give me a chance to get the notes from this cute guy named Harvey. He sits behind me."

I spit the water into the face bowl and wiped my mouth. "Atria, we need to stay focused here. Don't let a cute face turn into something like this," I told her, pointing to my stomach, "just like I did."

"I hear you, Nicole, I listens to everything you say to me—trust me."

And I believed her. That's one thing I loved about Atria—she was smart, attentive, and very outgoing, and she looked at me like I was a queen. When I talk to her, I don't see a family resemblance between her and Victor at all. They are like night and day.

She took the half-empty glass from my hand, walked into the kitchen, and placed it in the kitchen sink. She sat at the dining room table where her opened schoolbooks were waiting for her return. She placed her headphones on her head.

"If anybody calls for me, would you take a message? Just tell them that I'm resting," I hollered through the crack of my bedroom door. But she didn't respond.

I put my warm terry socks onto my feet, snuggled under my blanket, and got comfortable.

I stared at the digital clock on my dresser until my eyes were too heavy to keep open. I sensed the soothing smell of Darren's mystifying cologne in the air's breeze. As I eased into a deeper sleep, several thoughts of Darren's warm hands rubbing the small of my back made me more comfortable,and I was able to descend into a deep, peaceful, and serene state of mind. Within moments, I was out.

"Nicole…telephone," Atria whispered. The fluorescent numbers from the phone shined in my face as she began tapping my shoulders. "Nicole…telephone."

"What time is it?" I asked.

Atria stood over me with the phone in one hand and a French book in the other.

"8:53 p.m." she answered. "You've been asleep for two hours."

I sat up, took the phone from her hand, and covered the mouthpiece with my sweaty palms.

"You should have just told them I was sleeping," I whispered.

"It's Darren. You know—the man you've been wrecking your brain thinking about over the last several months?"

Darren had been on my mind a lot within the past three months. I wanted to call him on several occasions, but the fluttering human in my belly made me hesitant.

"Who?" I asked.

"Dar-ren," she pronounced two syllables.

"How did he—?" I scoffed.

Atria stood there shrugging her shoulders.

"And just how long have you and him been in there talking?" I brushed my hands against my eyes, wiping some of the sleep away.

She looked at her wristwatch and popped her tongue, "Um, I'd say about twenty minutes."

"That's too long to be talking to someone you don't even know, Atria."

"Oh, I know him. You talk about him so much, I was wondering when you were going to call him up and let him know that you are madly in love with him."

"I am not in love, so don't even go there."

"Yes you are; you just won't admit it." She triple-snapped her fingers in a zigzag motion, "Nah! All you have to do is put the phone to your ear and let him know."

"You didn't tell him I was five months pregnant, did you?" I whispered. "I'm not ready to tell him about the baby yet."

"Uh-uhn. Why would I do that? That is your job. I'm sure you'll tell him before the baby is born."

"Okay Atria, get out. You can leave now, and close the door behind you."

"By the way, Nicole. Chrystal said she'll be by in the morning to get some more of her clothes. She said she was going to stay at her mom's for another week."

"Fine. Close my door," I said to her.

Atria blew an imaginary kiss into the air before tiptoeing out the door. Then she closed it.

"How in the world did he get my number?" I asked myself. "That's what I'd like to know."

It was obvious how he got it. Darren worked for the police department. He can access any information he wanted to get on any person. He probably had my horrific life story and all my childhood police records in front of him right now. Ugh! That would be a mess.

I inhaled and exhaled before I lifted the phone to my ear.

"Hello?"

"Well hello, stranger. Did I catch you at a bad time?"

"Not really, I'm just trying to catch up on some sleep."

"Atria told me you were in your bedroom lying down; she didn't say anything about sleeping. You want me to call you back?"

"Nah! It's okay." It felt good to hear his voice. There was nervousness and excitement wrapped up in a ball and lodged in the center of my abdomen.

"Why are you so tired? Did you work hard at the hotel today?"

"Who told you I worked at the hotel?" I asked in surprise.

"Atria. She told me how she's been trying to get a job there, but her cousin wouldn't hire her." A brief moment of silence arose before he continued. "So I told her that I would talk to you and convince you to let her get her a job there."

Little did he know that I was not the cousin she was referring to.

"No, Darren, you won't have to do that. She's in college. And to me, college is more important than some bootlegged job."

"Sometimes the bootlegged jobs are the ones that lead us to having better futures."

"Well tell me this, Darren; how can a woman who works at a hotel make enough to support her kids?"

"Aight Nick, take out a dollar bill. Any type of bill will do. A one-dollar bill, five-dollar—doesn't matter." My body hesitated to move from the comfortable position I was in. But my heart encouraged me that it was going to be well worth taking this walk beside him into this conversation.

I walked over to the dresser and retrieved my purse. I sat back down on the bed and unzipped my pocketbook. While picking up the phone, I took one of the fifty-dollar bills from a bank withdrawal envelope and stared at Ulysses S. Grant's face before I continued.

"Okay, I got a $50 bill, now tell me what I'm looking for."

"Flip it over on the back and tell me what it says," he suggested.

I flipped it over and read the words aloud to him: "In God we trust."

"See Nicole, the money even tells you that you should put your faith in God and not in itself."

"Alrighty then," I confirmed.

"When you put your trust in the Lord—I mean really start trusting in him to do everything in your life—you start walking his walk, talking his talk; everything becomes like a breath of fresh air again. His protection is fulfilling. The bible says that even your enemies will become your footstool."

He had my ears open and receptive to all his opinions, suggestions and information. Darren said a lot of things that had my mind thinking on a whole new level. And for once in my life, my heart had begun to experience joy and a little peace—a healing process. Now I could actually feel my heart beating. He said a prayer before we said our goodnights. After we hung up, I sat quietly, wondering and praying about my life soon having a meaning to it. I wanted to be in a position where I could watch the sun rise and the moon set in an awe-inspiring display like I did when I was a kid. I just wanted to be able to let my fears and doubts go once again and to bring joy and peace back into my heart.

I made up my mind that it was time for this vicious cycle to stop.

For some crazy reason, God kept me here on his green-and-blue earth. I don't know what his purpose was, but my heart was telling me to listen to what Darren said instead of what my mother had been telling me for years.

"Search for things in your life that make your soul joyous," he said, "whether it's going bowling or watching the sunset on a bridge. Monitor your heart and pour positive thoughts into it. Then sit back and watch how good things turn out."

What did I have to lose by doing this? Starting tomorrow, I was determined to start my new walk.

Chapter Twenty-nine

"What Is He Staring At?"

*J*t was a sunny day, but the chill in the air made it a comfortable, jacket-wearing day. I was in the office talking to the hotel owner, Mr. Houston, about Victor's attitude. He told me that Victor was becoming irresponsible with his management duties and that he would give me a bonus if I stayed on him.

That was the kind of information I needed to hear.

"Okay, Mr. Houston, I'll see to it that Victor has those records on your desk as soon as possible," I told Mr. Houston. I had a huge grin on my face. I knew that when Victor walked back into the office, I would finally be allowed to point my fingers back into his face.

Victor walked in from his cigarette break right before I ended my conversation with our boss. He overheard the end of our conversation.

"What records are you talking about?" Victor said, barging into the office, "and have them on whose desk?"

I raised my index finger at him as a gesture to hold his thoughts. "Okay I sure will...you're welcome...bye," I said, and then I hung up.

"What records are you talking about? Who was that?" he repeated.

"Don't you know that it is rude to interrupt a business call?"

"Yeah, I know," he answered. "But what records are you talking about?"

"You don't remember the records, huh?" I said, pointing to the mess of papers on top of his desk. "The ones that started on your desk but walked over and sat on mine. Now they are back on your desk. Oh, and by the way, Mr. Houston said he will write you up if they aren't finished."

"Well, where are they?" he asked as he shuffled the papers around on his desk.

"Underneath your pile of junk." I pointed. I sat back in my chair, picked up my mug, and sipped my lemon tea with confidence. I was confident that I was able to check his ass and put him back in line.

He found them, picked them up, looked at them, walked over and slammed them onto my desk. "Didn't Mr. Houston tell you he wanted *you* to make sure they made it on his desk?"

"Mr. Houston gave that responsibility to you, not me. He made me responsible for staying on your back and making sure that you do it," I told him sarcastically. "So get to work."

"So it's like that, huh? I thought me and you was better than that. You know I'm swamped with stuff to do. Something like this would have only taken up ten minutes of your time. Ten minutes to go onto your computer and dock those calculations." Finally he found the book underneath the pile. He opened it and flipped through the pages.

"Ten minutes, huh?" I took a swig of my tea and gulped it. "Ah, let me see. That's about the same amount of time it took you to go smoke that cigarette, right?" I said to him, never making eye contact with him. "Listen, I got an interview to do right now. I suggest you have them done and faxed by the end of the day, so that you won't be in hot water."

"Oh my goodness." He slapped his hand on his chest. "Did somebody just mail you a backbone, or are the hormones trying to give orders now? Last time I checked, I was the boss in here."

"Last time I checked, you were the boss too. So why is Mr. Houston telling me to give you orders?" I got up from my seat and walked out of the office, Leaving Victor in the room with his mouth stupidly hanging open.

Before the interview ended, my stomach growled. An early lunch break was what I needed since most of my morning tasks were done.

Victor would usually go and get my lunch, but today I wanted his cousin Atria to join me outside of these hotel walls.

"Atria, this is Nicole. Are you busy?"

"Nope. I just got out of class and I'm starving."

"I'm about to take my lunch break; want to join me?" I asked.

"Franklin's Steak and Grill in ten minutes?" she properly asked.

"Franklin's Steak and Grill in ten minutes sound good to me," I said.

"All right then, Nick. Let's do the damn thang."

Then we hung up.

The flawless-skinned waitress escorted us to our booth. When we sat down, I noticed the waitress's oversized belly. I wanted to ask if she was pregnant, but I didn't want her to tell me that it was flab. So I didn't bother.

"Hello, ladies."

"Hi," We both said in harmony while smiling.

"My name is Rachel, and I'll be your server for today," She said while placing the menus on our empty table. "Can I get you ladies anything to drink?"

"Iced tea with lemon for me, please," I requested, putting my purse onto the booth's chair. Then I used my jacket to cover it.

"And for you?" Rachel asked Atria.

"I'll have the same," Atria stated.

"Two Iced teas with lemon coming right up." She turned around and began walking toward the kitchen, but Atria stopped her.

"Excuse me—Rachel, is it?" Atria asked.

"Yes," she enthusiastically answered.

"Are you pregnant?" Atria asked. I hid my face in my menu in embarrassment.

"Yes I am."

"How many months are you, Rachel?"

"I'm in my seventh month," Rachel said while rubbing her oval-shaped belly.

"Are you even supposed to be working when you're that many months pregnant?" Atria asked.

"Not really," she answered, "but somebody has to make the money."

Atria pointed her finger at my stomach. "Well, she's seven months too."

"Are you really?" Rachel asked me.

"Yeah. Well, I'm almost seven months," I shyly answered.

"Wow, you look so much smaller than I do. I didn't want to ask; I thought it was just flab," she explained. She kept the smile on her face as she continued. "This is me and Victor's second child. I've carried both of them big."

"Wait a minute, did you say Victor?" Atria interrupted. "What is his last name?"

Rachel stared at Atria with a confused look on her face before answering.

"Falcon. His name is Victor Falcon." Her eyes widened and her eyebrows lifted. Her hand cupped her mouth as she spoke. "You're not his wife are you?"

"Oh, no. I'm definitely not married to a Victor." My voice rose uncontrollably.

"Neither am I." Rachel chuckled "But for every man that's an asshole, there is at least three good men around him."

"You're pregnant with a married man's baby. How did that happen?" Atria folded her arms and propped them on the table. She was curiously staring into Rachel's face without blinking.

"Long story. But to sum it all up, his triflin' ass forgot to tell me that he got married." She placed a big checkmark on our check. "I'll be right back with your drinks, okay?"

"Okay," we both said in unison.

Atria and I both shook our heads in shame. We both knew it was the same Victor who had fathered my child. How obvious was that? And just how many Victor Falcons could there possibly be that are spreading themselves around like this? I'd already accepted the fact that Victor was not a real man. Otherwise, I would have called him from my cell and given the phone to Rachel just to start some trouble.

Atria leaned back in her chair with her hands cupped over her mouth.

"My cousin is a whore," she said. "I have met a lot of Victor's girlfriends, but never have I seen that one before."

"I know. Just lay low until we find out more information. We don't know for sure if we are talking about the same Victor."

Atria raised her arm like a child in a classroom, "Um…am I the only one who can see clear here?"

I didn't answer.

"Nicole, if you knew of a man who was involved with another woman, why would you sleep with him?"

"I have to use the restroom, Atria. I'll be right back." I rose to my feet and grabbed my purse.

"Nicole, I'm sorry."

"Just forget about it,"

Atria's head lowered in disappointment. Disappointed for saying something that she obviously didn't mean to say.

"You want me to order the usual steak? Or are you having the chicken and fettuccini noodles?"

"Chicken," I answered. "And tell Rachel not to put garlic on it, will you?"

"Garlic?" Her face was distraught.

"Yes garlic."

"Don't you need it to keep off evil spirits?"

We both laughed as I excused myself from the table, I wobbled my way into the restroom and found an available stall. As I washed my hands in the sink, I stared into the mirror, wondering if I had been making the right decisions in my life. I closed my eyes.

"Lord, please refresh my spirit," I said.
And so it was.

Victor will get exactly what he deserves. We all will. There was no need for me to try to get revenge on him or anyone else. We all have to pay for our unrighteous acts. So who am I to try and shoot him down. Darren quotes "God said even your enemies will become your footstool."

Wiping the tears from my eyes, I walked out the bathroom door feeling uplifted and refreshed. I sat down at the table where the steam from the chicken fettuccini noodles were rising from my plate.

"Thank God the service here is fast, because I am starving," I said to my lunch date, who had already started working through her vegetables. She looked up and stared into my eyes.

"You been crying, haven't you?"

"No. I'm fine. Mind your business." I said my grace, picked my fork up, and began stirring the sauce into the noodles.

"Your eyes are red," she said, "and your face look puffy."

"I'm pregnant, Atria; enjoy your food. I have to get back to work soon. I got to have a talk with Victor."

Atria hunched her shoulders. And without a second thought, she began eating again.

She looked up and paused. "I know I be hungry when I first get in a restaurant, but staring at someone who is already eating is considered being rude."

"What are you talking about?" I asked before blowing into my steamy, noodlefilled fork.

"That guy sitting over there." She nodded toward the person. "He was just staring at you when you came out of the restroom. And now he's staring harder."

"Just ignore him," I demanded. I didn't turn around. My food was calling me. I didn't care whether or not someone was staring over me or sitting on my lap; I just wanted to eat.

"I would ignore him if he wasn't so fine, though." She ate the small portion of steak from her fork and froze. "Um, Nick, now I think he's trying to get your attention."

If I didn't turn around to see who it was, Atria would have kept talking about him.

I took a quick look behind me, then turned back around.

"Uh oh."

Atria threw her body forward against the table and leaned her ears toward me. "Uh oh what?"

"Atria—that's Darren."

"Darren?" She looked over my shoulder again, flashed him an all-teeth smile, and gave him a wave. "Well, what are you waiting for? Tell Darren to come over so I can meet him."

"I would, but you see there's a slight problem."

"A slight problem? What the hell kind of slight problem?"

"I never told him I was pregnant."

"Well, he knows it now. How long did you think you were going to hide that belly of yours, Nicole? Plus he saw yo' big ass wobbling in from the restroom."

"I am not ready to tell him about the baby. He is going to think I am playing games," I told her.

Atria shook her head shamelessly. "So who did you think you were going to hurt by telling him the truth, Nicole? Now you are on lockdown. Now you're forced to do it."

Damn. She was right. It was too late to hide it. I had to come clean and give him an explanation. The question now was, how would I do it?

I dropped my fork onto my plate and dabbed my mouth with the napkin. "You think I should go over and talk to him, or tell him to come over here?" I nervously asked.

"It doesn't matter now," she answered, taking a swig of her lemon iced tea and placing it back onto the table.

"Why doesn't it matter anymore, Atria?" I asked in frustration. "Did he leave out of the restaurant?"

"Nope, he didn't," she answered, taking another bite of her vegetables and chewing it hysterically.

"Well, why is it too late?"

"'Cause he is standing right behind you."

As soon as she said it, the hairs on the back of my neck stood up like a black man at a strip joint.

So now what do I do?

My eyes were locked onto a flower-shaped parsley flake from my plate. I wanted Darren to say something to me first. But he didn't. He sat next to me in the booth, tucked my hair behind my ear, and brushed the back of his hand against my face. He leaned over, pressing his warm lips against my cheek, and gave me the softest kiss. He laid one hand on my stomach.

"When were you going to tell me about the baby?" Darren softly asked.

"Um...I...uh..."

"If you told me that you were involved with someone, I would have understood."

I looked over at Atria, who was guiding me with her eyes to tell the truth. The truth about how much I liked Darren. And how I was trying to make the right decisions with the baby without putting our relationship in jeopardy. I just thought the timing was off.

"Sir, should I bring your dinner to this table?" Rachel interrupted.

Atria looked at Darren, Darren looked at me, and then I looked at Atria before Darren cleared his throat and spoke. "Since I'm already here, why not?"

"Yes Rachel, he will be joining us for dinner," Atria answered.

"I like Darren, but is he for real?" I asked.
And the questions were being answered

I didn't feel like going back to work after lunch. It was my turn to take days off whenever I felt like it. And right now, I felt like it.

Darren and I spent the rest of the day together after Atria went her separate way. We went for ice cream at a nearby parlor and a walk in the park. We talked, we laughed, and we held hands. He is quite a gentleman. And can you believe he took me to Chin Lou's Nail Salon for a manicure and a pedicure while he patiently sat and watched?

Did it feel funny holding hands with a man while pregnant with another man's child? Yes!

But I didn't care. And neither did he. We spent most of the day talking about the baby so much that it almost felt like it was his. Did Darren come into my life in the nick of time or what?

Chapter Thirty

"Who's The Boss?"

$\mathcal{I}$ was walking through the hotel's corridors on a warm and sunny Monday morning, feeling confident. I could hear Victor's wife, Daniece, screaming at the top of her lungs. This was unusual for a woman like Daniece. She was not the type of woman that brings chaos to her man's office like this. Today was different. Daniece must have heard about Rachel. I thought I would go in and find out.

My lovely lips parted into a smile as I walked through the door. I had waited a long time to see someone whup Victor's ass.

I grabbed my fingernail file from my desk drawer and sat in my chair. By this time, Daniece was standing over Vic, holding the picture frame I bought him for Christmas above his head.

This would be well worth my time. To see her crack it over his head right now would do me a lot of justice. If she didn't do it, I would be happy to do it for her. I sat back in my chair and made myself invisible, watching them continue on Daniece's journey to reconstitution.

"Vic, are you going to tell me who the hell this Rachel chic is?And why is she filing for child support?"

"Child support? C'mon Daniece. Where is your proof?"

Daniece tossed the frame onto the desk. She reached inside of her briefcase and pulled out a manila envelope before tossing it on the desk, in front of Victor. Victor picked it up and glanced in my direction with worried eyes.

"Well don't look at me," I mumbled, focusing my attention on my freshly manicured hands.

179

"Victor Thomas Falcon III," Daniece shouted, "Who the hell is Rachel?"

"I'm for real baby; I don't know who that is." He rose from his chair. "Look baby, why don't you go on home and calm down, and we can discuss this when I get home."

"No, I don't want to wait, Victor. I need to know now."

"I don't know why you tripping. You know I'm named after my father. These things happen all the time."

"That is a bunch of bull, Victor. When are you going to stop lying to me?" she asked. She threw her head back, turned around and slammed her fist against the wall.

"I am not lying to you baby. I need you to trust me, Daniece. You know I love you," Vic said as he escorted her toward the door. "Just relax. Let me call the Friend of the Court office and straighten this out. I'm sure this whole thing is just a mistake."

"You better hope so. Not for my sake, but for yours." With that, she walked out, slamming the door behind her.

I felt sorry for him. His eyes sunk into the front cover in silence before opening the envelope. He pulled the child support forms out and tossed the envelope on the desk. He looked up at me, then down at the papers.

"Nicole?" he asked.

"What?" I said, blowing my nails as if they were wet.

"I'm sorry I've been rough on you lately."

"Mm-hm," I mumbled. "And I'm all burnt out from doing favors for you, Victor. So don't ask me for one."

"I'm not going to ask you for a favor."

I picked up a magazine from my desk and began flipping pages.

"Can you keep a secret?" he asked.

I scoffed. "I thought that's what I've been doing for the last seven months."

The room was so still and silent that I could hear the crickets coming from his head.

"Well, can you like continue to keep that secret?"

I jumped up from my seat and placed my index finger in his face. "To hell with you, Victor. I knew you were going to do something like this. You want to know something? My baby and I don't need your sorry ass anyway. I got a man. A saved one. And he is willing to take on your responsibilities. So if you think for one second you are going to ruin this child's life like you did your own, you have really lost your mind. And don't think that I am going to kiss your ass or ask you for any child support, because I don't need that either. You shouldn't have to be forced to take care of your own business. So as far as I am concerned, you are a nobody—to me and the baby."

I walked out the door. I had no idea how I was going to support this kid on my own, but I had faith in God that everything was going to work out. And I believed that.

Later on that evening, Victor received a phone call from our boss Mr. Houston. He told Victor that he was fired from the hotel. Rachel's children were genetically proven to be Victor's. His wife, Daniece, kicked him out and filed for a divorce.

What happened to Victor after that? No one knows or cares. However, Christyl and I are now the new manager and assistant manager of the hotel.

And guess who the Boss is...ME!

Chapter Thirty-one

"All Things Will Work Together For The Good."

The night was young, the moon was glowing, and the air was breezy. The moment snuck upon me like a thief in the night. It was time—time for the labor pains, the agony, the frustrations, and the light of bringing forth another life into the world. Today, God spoke. He said that I was indeed ready to become a mother—the product of reproduction.

And I was ready. I had to be. There was no other choice but to be ready. My water had broken and I was indeed ready to push this child out of my womb and into the cold phases of the world.

Darren—my sweetheart Darren—was on his way to the apartment. I had been sitting on the phone and talking to him for an hour when the labor process began. After we ended our phone conversation, He was here within ten minutes.

"Are you ready to do this?" he asked, grabbing my coat and placing it on my shoulders. I was packed and ready. I grabbed my boyfriend's hand, locked the door, and was on my way to the hospital.

I thought about my mother the whole time. I wanted to know where she began thinking that my life would be a waste. Was it at birth? That couldn't be. Because the only question that a mother could think of at a time like this was, is my baby going to be healthy, strong, and with all senses so that she could lead a normal life?

I pushed and I pushed my little baby girl into the world. My mind was racing and my thoughts floated abroad, I knew that there was no turning back. All I could think of was all the success this child will, would, and could have if I could just hold on to faith's hand.

I named her Destiny Victorya Lewis. She weighed 7 lbs, 6 oz. Her name meant *victorious destination*. It was self-explanatory. That name meant a lot to me. I wanted my daughter to have a victorious journey, a happy life, and a firm foundation from the start.

Isis, where are you? I thought as I heard my baby girl' cry. I couldn't think of any reason she had been ignoring my calls. I had left several messages letting her know that she had a grandchild processing and ready to be born any day. I made my final call before I left the apartment to inform her of which hospital I was going to just in case she decided to come.

I hadn't heard from her. But yet, I hadn't given up like she had with me. I wanted her to see her grandchild just as much as I wanted to see my baby brother or sister.

There I was, sitting in the labor and delivery recovery room, holding my beautiful little girl. Her nose was tiny and her head was petite. I hoped that this child was going to be much smarter and wiser than I was and that she would do much greater things than her mother and her no-good father ever did. This child was going to be a genius—or so I hoped.

Finally, the nurse walked in with a guest. "Ms. Lewis, someone is here to see you."

I asked, "Who is it?"

My mother, Isis, walked in with contentment on her face. Her hands were attached to a cute little boy that looked similar to my baby picture.

"Go say hello, Armani. Go ahead." He shrugged his shoulders as Isis slowly guided him into my direction. His arms spread out wide, waiting for a hug. I embraced him in my arms and held him tightly. This was my little brother, and I didn't want to let him go. Finally, after the long journey of wondering whether it was a boy or girl and worrying about his well being, he was in my arms.

He scooted onto the bed. "You are my big sister, Nicole, aren't you?" He said. His eyelashes batted together and curved into his eyebrows as they opened. His face reminded me of a baby cub cuddling under its mother.

"Yes," I said, "and you are my little brother, Armani, aren't you?" I tapped his little nose and tickled his belly. His laughter burst into the air, filling it with joy. My mother took a seat in the chair beside my hospital bed, placing one leg over the other. She had never looked so pretty in her life. Her hair, nails, and toes were freshly manicured. Her make up was flawless, and her eyes were glowing like the moonlit sky. She smiled delightfully without saying a word. Her vibes were evident and spoke for themselves. They whispered peace and understanding, joy and comfort.

"How old are you?" I asked Armani. I already knew the answer, but I wanted to hear it from him.

"Four." He held up four fingers, all of them tiny, soft, and brittle. His eyes were glossy, wide, and confident, like they'd seen a lot and been in this world before.

Isis shifted in her chair. Finally, she spoke. Her words were gentle, and they flowed gracefully from her motherly lips.

"You're going to make a good mother, Nicole," she humbly encouraged. She reached within her purse and pulled out a rectangle-shaped box—a pink one. "This is for you and the baby."

I embraced the gift before loosening the pink ribbon. I unwrapped the paper and then pulled out its contents. I was shocked at what I saw. My eyes became as big as saucers; my mouth dropped like my braless, milk-filled breasts.

I gasped.

My mother cleared her throat. "Ten thousand dollars; go ahead and count it; it's all there."

"But I only had—"

"I know how much was in the mattress," she said politely. "After Harold mysteriously came up missing, I invested the money you had in the mattress in my restaurant. After some hard work and dedication and praying, I was able to earn your money back. I will give you the papers to sign later."

"Papers?" I curiously asked. "What papers?"

"The papers to your share of the royalties. You will take over the restaurant just in case something happens to me. In the meantime, you get a good percentage of the profits."

"Oh!" I pleasurably concurred. "You did not have to do this."

"Yes I did. I wouldn't have been able to open it if it wasn't for you telling me how much I can cook...and your investments, of course."

This was a dream come true. It felt like I hit a multimillion jackpot. It's amazing how God shows up when we least expect it. I knew I needed to buy things for the baby, but didn't know how. And look how everything worked out in the nick of time.

"You opened a restaurant?"

"I sure did," she said, nodding her head up and down. "Isis's Soul Food Palace—that's the name of it."

That was good news. Not the part about Harold mysteriously disappearing, but the news about her opening a restaurant.

I was curious, though. Did Papa G have something to do with it, or did Jet-Money knock him off? This was yet to be discovered, but now was not the time.

"Congratulations." Tears rolled down my cheek in her honor.

"Thank you," she obliged.

I looked over at my sleeping newborn who was in her glass bassinet. I picked her up, tucking the receiving blanket around her little body.

"This is your grandchild, Destiny Victorya. Destiny, this is your grandmother, Isis."

Armani took Destiny's hand into his. "Is she my sister too?"

"No sweetie, this is your niece," Isis announced, taking Destiny into her arms. "She will call you Uncle Armani."

"Uncle Armani?" he delightfully repeated. "I like that."

Darren walked in. His eyes lit up like a kid on the Forth of July when he saw Isis and Armani. Armani jumped from the bed and drew out his hand for a handshake. "Hi."

"'What's up little man. What's your name?" Darren asked, accepting his handshake.

"Armani. What's yours?"

"Darren," he answered. "How old are you, Armani?"

"Four." This time he flexed his arms, proving his boyish muscles. "I'm four."

"Darren, I'm Isis." She took his hand upon hers and lowered her head. "Congratulations. You have a beautiful daughter."

Darren accepted her handshake. He was in total amazement. He wasn't expecting my devilishly talking mother to congratulate him on someone else's child, but he was happy to take the credit.

"Thank you, Ms. Isis," he replied. "And you have a beautiful daughter as well."

Our eyes met. Darren leaned over, placing his lips against mine, leaving traces of his love upon my lips. "Did Nicole tell you the good news?"

"What good news?" Isis asked.

"Nicole and I are getting married." He took a black box from his shirt pocket and placed it in my hands. I was stunned.

"Open it baby. It's for you."

Unbelievable. God's timing is unbelievable. The whole moment was absolutely beautiful. And guess what? It was the same ring I had showed him and told him I liked. This was the one that was in the store when I was with Christyl. It was a ten-karat white gold diamond princess cut ring with baguettes. The Chinese lady must "a bring-a-hem a good deal, yeah."

Christyl peeked her head inside the door. "Knock, knock. Can I come in?" she asked.

Darren answered by saying, "You came just in time. Nicole was about to—"

"Oh my God, Nick, that is Beautiful!"

Before Darren could complete his sentence, Chris dropped the big yellow gift bag onto the wooden floor and dropped her jaw. She walked over slowly and grabbed the hand with the ring on it.

"He just asked me," I said, smiling from ear to ear.

Chris balled her fists up and placed them on her hips. "And what did you say?"

"Nicole hasn't given an answer yet," Isis said. "We are still waiting on it."

Christyl slapped her hand over her mouth and gave Isis a hug. "I'm sorry Ms. Isis; I didn't mean to be rude."

"It's okay, Chris." Isis hugged her back. "I didn't mean to be rude to you at the mall."

"It's okay. I had to step away to let you and Nicole work things out." Chris angelically forgave her in her heart. I thought that was cool of her to do.

"That diamond is taking up all the attention in the room. How long do we have to wait on the answer?" My mother asked.

"Yeah Nick, it is huge," Chris said as she placed her fists back onto her hips. "So this automatically makes me a godmother of Destiny, and a maid of honor in the wedding, right?"

"Yes, Chris." I stared into Darren's deep brown eyes, gently placing my lips upon his. "I say yes."

About the Author

La Sonya Jones-Lamine was born in Detroit and graduated from Cooley High School. At the age of 8, her mother and father discovered her talent in writing. Since then, she has written several short stories, poems, and documentaries. ...In The Nick Of Time is her first published novel. La Sonya now lives with her husband and thier two daughters.

Coming soon ...In the Nick of Times 2.

Breinigsville, PA USA
25 March 2011
258406BV00001B/46/A